D0389608

Mom Is Dating Weird Wayne

MARY JANE AUCH

Mom Is Dating Weird Wayne

HOLIDAY HOUSE / NEW YORK

Library of Congress Cataloging-in-Publication Data

Auch, Mary Jane.
Mom is dating weird Wayne.

Summary: Jenna objects to her mother's new boyfriend,
a wacky weatherman, and exerts every effort to prevent
his becoming her new father.
[1. Single-parent family--Fiction] I. Title.
PZ7.A898Mo 1988   [Fic]   88-45275
ISBN 0-8234-0720-9

For **HERM** and **IAN**—
the men in my life.

Mom Is Dating Weird Wayne

CHAPTER 1

Right in the middle of math class, Randy Schloss tapped on my shoulder and handed me a note. I almost didn't take it because Randy Schloss is about the last person in the world I'd want to get a note from, but I noticed the familiar triangular fold and knew it had to be from Molly. I propped my math book up on my desk and opened the note behind it so Mr. Bartholomew wouldn't see me reading it.

> Dear Jenna,
> How would you like your future name to be Jenna Bartholomew? I have a *great* plan. I'll tell you all about it at lunch. Your troubles are over!!!
>
> > Love,
> > Molly

That was typical Molly. Each year since fourth grade she'd fallen in love with every handsome new male teacher in school. This year, in seventh, there were two of them, Mr. Hastings and Mr. Bartholomew. She must have decided Mr. Bartholomew could be mine. He was handsome enough, but I had bigger things to worry about than whether or not to fall in love, especially with a math teacher, for pete's sake. What would we have in common? Math was my worst subject.

The bell rang, and Molly was next to my desk in a flash. "Hurry up. We have a lot to talk about."

"If this is another one of your brilliant plots, Molly, leave me out. You can get all gooney-eyed over Mr. B., but not me."

"Shhh. Do you want the world to know about this?" Molly rolled her eyes in the direction of Kimberly Stickle, who was practically a professional gossip.

"Quit shoving, will you?" I growled. Molly had propelled me down the hall and to the cafeteria. She was aiming me toward the table in the corner where nobody sat because it was next to the big garbage can. "Can't we sit at our regular table? This one stinks."

"I know. This way we won't be interrupted." Molly raised her eyebrows. "I don't think you'll want anybody to hear this."

I dug into my lunch bag and pulled out a peanut butter sandwich that looked like a lump of play-dough. My social studies book had fallen on it in my locker. I sure missed the days when I could take my old Snow White lunch box to school. My sandwiches never got mushed up then, but I stopped doing that in fifth grade. Even the nerds didn't carry lunch boxes in seventh.

"I have the answer to all your problems," Molly said, waving a celery stick like a magic wand.

"Great. You're going to zap my father back here from Colorado, and he's going to divorce his new wife and remarry my mother, right? Then we'll all move into a castle and live happily ever after until my sixteenth birthday, when I'll prick my finger and fall asleep for a hundred years. Then one day Mr. Bartholomew will find me, kiss me, and I'll wake up. Of course he'll be a lot older then, so he won't be such a great catch anymore."

Molly was tapping her fingers on the table. "Have you run out of smart remarks now, so we can get on with this before the bell rings?"

I knew Molly wouldn't give up until I listened. "Sure. I'm just dying to hear your big plan." I broke off a little ball of play-dough and popped it into my mouth. It tasted as good as it looked.

"This came to me in a flash, right in the middle of class," Molly said. Things were always coming to Molly in a flash in the middle of class, which is why she got D's in three out of five subjects last year. "Mr. Bartholomew would make a perfect husband. He's new in town, and you have to admit he's the handsomest teacher we've had yet. If we really get going, I'll bet we could be hearing wedding bells by spring. What do you think?"

This was the big plan? "Listen, Molly, I hate to spoil all your fun, but I promised Mom I wouldn't get married until I was at least in eighth grade."

Molly glared at me. "Sure, make jokes, but while you're wasting time trying to be funny, somebody else is going to snatch him up, and your poor mother will lose out on getting a great-looking new husband."

"My mother and Mr. B? About the last thing Mom needs right now is a new husband. She says she's still recovering from the old one."

"Did you or did you not tell me your mother was going nuts trying to pay all the bills? Hasn't she had about six different jobs since the divorce?"

"She's just trying to find out what she does best. Maybe she's not a big-deal executive like your mom, but we're getting along just fine."

That was a lie. Mom had been fired from one job after another in the past few months, and it wasn't because she didn't try. Sometimes she tried too hard, like on her first day working at Bennie's Beanery. She tried to carry two trays full of glasses at once and dropped everything. Mom couldn't help it. She just wasn't good at earning a living.

To make matters worse, I knew Dad wasn't coming through with the support payments every month, so things were getting a bit tight. It wasn't really Dad's fault, though. Gladys, his new wife, was spending all of his money. He probably didn't make that much, anyway, selling chemical toilets for recreational vehicles. I wished Molly could wave a magic wand and zap Dad back. It was taking too long for him to come to his senses. I knew Gladys was a money-grubber the first time I saw her modeling at the RV show in Rochester. She was wearing enough jewelry to sink a canoe—at least one ring on each finger and about five pierced earrings on each ear. Her bangly gold bracelets kept getting caught in the zipper of the screen house she was trying to demonstrate.

"Jenna!"

"Mmm?"

"Quit daydreaming, will you? I'm not putting your Mom down. I think she's the most talented mother I've ever met. Remember when she used to be a clown and go around to visit kids in hospitals? She's artistic, too. I loved all those wall hangings she made with the melted wax and dyes, and she made the best Halloween costumes in the whole neighborhood."

"Yeah," I mumbled. "Too bad she can't turn that into a career."

"Why couldn't she?" Molly slammed her celery stick down on the table so hard it broke in half. "That's a great idea."

"It's a little hard to support a family by working just one day a year, Molly."

"But it's a way your Mom could earn some extra money. Halloween's only a few weeks away. She could put an ad in the paper for doing scary make-up for people."

"Oh sure, what would she get? Twenty-five cents for each kid she did?"

"Not kids—adults. Mom and Dad go to a big costume party every Halloween at the country club. They spend a mint on their costumes, and I bet they'd pay a lot for a professional makeup job. I know my mom hates to wear a mask."

I gave up on my sandwich and squished it into a little ball. "It might not be a bad idea. I'll tell her about it tonight." At least it sounded more sensible than having Mom marry Mr. Bartholomew. Molly seemed to have the idea that everyone and everything should have a mate. Even the Welter's animals came in pairs—two cats, two parakeets, and two goldfish. Uneven numbers made Molly nervous.

"Now, getting back to your mom and Mr. Bartholomew. Just make sure she looks really good next week when you come to open house. She has to make an impression. Does she have a really sexy dress?"

"My mother? Are you kidding? I'm not even sure she owns a dress, except for her waitress uniform, and I think she had to give that back. She always wears jeans and sweats and stuff."

"Maybe my mother has something. They're about the same size. Come over to my house after school, and we'll look through her closet."

I wasn't taking any handouts from Molly, even if she meant well. I'd always known Molly's family had more money than ours, but it never mattered that much before. We even lived on the same street, before we sold the house and moved into an apartment. "I can't do anything after school. Mom started a new job today, and I have to pick up Corey at the elementary school and watch him until she comes home."

"Bring him along, and we'll both watch him."

"Can't. I have to make dinner. Mom's always starved after the first day on a new job."

"A new job? Don't tell me your mother's starting in on something else, Jenna. What new field is she ... breaking ... into this time?" It was Kimberly Stickle. She could eavesdrop on a conversation a half mile away, then sneak up without being heard.

"It's none of your business what my mother does," I mumbled.

Kimberly sidled up closer to our table. "I guess it is my business if you go on welfare and we tax-payers have to support you. My daddy says that welfare money comes right out of our pockets."

"Nobody's going on welfare," I said. "Mom and Corey and I are . . ."

Molly stood up and tossed her half-empty milk carton so it hit the side of the garbage can, splattering milk down the front of Kimberly's skirt.

"You idiot! Look what you've done," Kimberly shrieked.

"Sorry, Kimberly. I didn't see you standing next to that garbage can. You sort of blended right in."

I stifled a snort and tried to keep a straight face. Kimberly grabbed Molly's napkin and started dabbing at the skirt as she headed back to her table. "You're paying the cleaning bill for this, Molly Welter," she yelled over her shoulder. "You too, Jenna. You're just as bad as she is."

"Pull some of that welfare money out of your pocket to pay for it," Molly shouted. "That's where all that money comes from, you know. Right out of your pocket."

"Thanks, Molly," I said after we settled back down at the table. "I probably would have gotten into a big argument with her, and she always wins."

"Hey, what are friends for? Now, let's get back to the wedding plans."

But before Molly could say anything else, the bell rang.

CHAPTER 2

Corey was waiting in front of the elementary school when I got there. He looked so little, hunched up under his backpack.

"Hi, sport. How was your day?"

"Okay," he mumbled, grabbing my hand.

I watched a bunch of boys kicking an old soccer ball around on the playground as we cut over toward our street. "Those kids look about your age. Any of them in your first-grade class?"

Corey kept his eyes on the sidewalk. "No."

Just then the ball rolled across our path, and a chubby little kid practically tripped over my feet trying to get it. He picked it up and turned back to us. "Hey, Corey, wanna play?"

Corey ducked his head even more and shook it.

Another kid ran over. "Yeah, be on my team, and the sides will be even."

Corey was shrinking down so much I thought he

was going to slip through the crack in the sidewalk.

"Go ahead, Corey. I'll go home and come back to pick you up in a little while. I'll even take your backpack." I started to slip one strap off his shoulder.

"No!" Corey yanked the strap back up and grabbed my wrist, dragging me toward the gate that marked the end of the school property.

"Okay, okay. I get the message." I shook loose from his sticky little hand.

We crossed the road and walked along in silence, around the corner and past three houses to home. I fished the house key out of the small change purse Mom had pinned inside my back pack. While I jiggled the key around in the lock, Corey stood next to me, leaning slightly into my side. He reminded me of our dog Jaspar, waiting for me to open a can of dog food—trying to be patient but ready to spring as soon as it was opened. Jaspar must have been doing the same thing on the other side of the door because he nearly knocked us over as we tried to get inside. He was part sheep dog and part something else. You couldn't tell what because all the clues were hidden under his shaggy gray coat, except where Mom had cut his bangs so he could see better. Now the hair stuck out like the visor on a baseball cap. I managed to squeeze past Jaspar, but he had Corey pinned against the stair banister, plastering him with big sloppy kisses.

"Get off me, Jaspar." Corey's chin was stretched up as far as he could get it. Jaspar gave up on his face and started working on his neck. "Make him stop, Jenna."

Corey was giggling, so I didn't pay much attention to his cries for help. I scooped a few envelopes off the floor by the mail slot, hoping to find one from Dad. He hadn't written to me since last summer. That's when he told me he and Gladys would be away the whole month of August, so I couldn't go out to visit him the way we'd planned. There wasn't even an envelope addressed to Mom with his support check in it today. Just a bunch of junk addressed to "occupant" and a few bills.

"Jenna, help!" Corey wailed, his giggles turning to sobs.

I lifted him out of Jaspar's range. "Come on. He's just glad to see you. The poor mutt's been cooped up all day." Corey wriggled out of my arms, turned on the TV, and burrowed into the cushions on the couch.

Jaspar turned his attention to me, shoving me toward the kitchen door. I grabbed his leash and took him around to the back yard, then let him loose. Mom said we were lucky to find an apartment that had a fenced-in yard for a dog. We had to share it with Vincent, the man who lived in the rear apartment, but he never used it. He played in a band at night and slept most of the day until he got up to practice. He was a drummer, and when he really got going, he could make the whole house vibrate. When we first moved in, Molly had had this great idea about Mom marrying the mysterious musician next door—until she saw him. Vincent didn't fit Molly's image of Mr. Wonderful. He had long hair and a beard, and Molly said he probably hadn't come in contact with a comb or brush in years.

Jaspar was darting around the yard trying to decide where to do his business, which was stupid because he always did it in the same place. Then, when he did find the spot, the far corner of the yard by the neighbor's garage, he had to turn around about three dozen times to get the angle just right. "Come on, Jaspar. Just get this over with, will you?" I was tempted to leave him shut up in the yard, but Mom had found some holes in the fence that looked big enough for him to squeeze through.

I heard Vincent start in on the drums, and I felt a pang of homesickness for our big old house on Castlebar Road, where everything was always peaceful. Even though we'd moved only four blocks from our old neighborhood, it was like another world. Most of the houses on Russell Street were divided into apartments, and every weekend someone was moving in or out. Dad never would have let us live in a place like this. If he saw it, he'd make us move to a better neighborhood.

The dog was still searching for the perfect spot. "I'm giving up on you, Jaspar. You don't have a prayer of finding a hole in the fence if you can't find your own stupid bathroom." I made sure the gate was locked and went back into the house.

Corey met me at the door, in tears again. Vincent's playing was coming through the dining room wall loud and clear. "Somebody's banging in the walls. It's that monster who lives inside the walls, Jenna."

"It's the man next door, Corey. I've told you that about a million times."

"No, it's in our house. It's in the walls. I want Mommy. If she was home all the time, the monster couldn't get in here."

Since this house was about the size of our old house, Corey couldn't understand that it was divided into two apartments, one in front and one in back. Lately, it was hard to explain anything to him. He was scared of everything and everybody but Mom and me. I turned the TV up louder to drown out the drums, then went back to the kitchen to see what I had to do for supper.

There was a hamburger and macaroni casserole in the refrigerator with a note on it: "Put this in a 350 degree oven at 4:30 and make a salad." It was already 4:15, so I preheated the oven and started cutting up the vegetables. I tried to saw through a tomato with a dull paring knife. First it only made a deep crease in the tomato skin, but then it broke through, spewing tomato seeds all over my good sweater. I dabbed at the seeds with a paper towel, but they clung to the curly little hairs on the wool. Now I'd probably get yelled at for not changing my clothes as soon as I got home.

I missed the days when I could just hang out with Molly after school until Mom called us for dinner. Of course, some nights Mom would be cooking stew on one burner and hot wax for batik wall hangings on another, but she always managed to get something on the table. When a lot of the other mothers in the neighborhood were getting jobs to "fulfill themselves," Mom was content to sit home and mess around with her art projects. That's probably why she was so bad at earning a living. She'd never given it much thought before.

Even when Mom sold one of her wall hangings, she'd usually blow the money on something silly— a boat trip down the canal for all of us, or once a dinner in a fancy restaurant that rotated on top of a

tall building in Rochester. She always said the
money she earned was "just gravy." Now the gravy
was all we had.

A car pulled into the driveway next door, and I
saw a man with a briefcase coming home from
work. I remembered how I used to run out and
meet Dad every day and carry his briefcase in for
him. Then he'd have a cup of coffee with a little
milk in it, and I'd have a cup of milk with a little
coffee in it, and we'd read the paper together. Dad
always gave me the comics.

I was just going to fix myself a cup of milk with a
little coffee, for old time's sake, when I heard a
commotion on the front porch. Mom burst through
the door, loaded down with groceries, while Jaspar
jumped up on her. Darn! He must have found a
hole in the fence. I grabbed his collar and held him
while Mom chased after the apples that had rolled
all over the front hall. Jaspar managed to get hold
of one, and was chewing on it, dropping little bits
of apple skin on the floor.

"How did Jaspar get loose? You didn't leave him
in the yard, did you?"

"I'm sorry, Mom. I meant to get right back for
him, but I forgot."

"Jenna, I count on you to be responsible. Did
you get the casserole in the oven?"

I realized the oven had been preheating for half

an hour with nothing in it. "It's going in right now, Mom, and the salad's almost ready. I'm sorry, I should have put it in sooner, but..."

Mom glared at me for a second, then came over and hugged me. "Oh, it's all right, honey. You have a lot on your shoulders lately, but maybe things are going to work out for us from now on."

"Really? You like the new job? What are you doing, anyway?"

Mom put down the groceries and sat at the kitchen table. "Well, I told you I'm working at Class Memories. That's the company that takes school pictures all over the country."

"You don't go out and take the pictures, do you?"

"No, I work in the plant in the retouching department. They call us 'zit zappers.'"

"You're kidding!"

"The official company title is 'spotters,' but the girls I work with came up with the name. Kind of catchy, don't you think?"

"That's putting it mildly." If Kimberly Stickle got wind of this, she'd make my life miserable. "What does a zit zapper do?"

"Well, when there's a picture of a child with a pimple on his face, they take it off from the negative, but it shows up on the final print as a white spot. I have to mix flesh-colored dye and fill in the spot so you can't see it. It's fun, really. At least I'm

using some of my art school training in matching
the skin tones. Did you know some people even
have a greenish cast to their skin?"

"Hey, speaking of green skin, Mom, do you remember when you did that great Halloween
makeup for Corey, making him look like Yoda?"

"Sure. That was pretty good, wasn't it. You have
any ideas for this year? Halloween's getting close."

"I don't know about Corey and me, but Molly
said her parents always go to this fancy costume
party at the country club, and she thought you
could earn some extra money by doing makeup for
adults. You could put an ad in the paper."

Mom looked sad for a minute. "The whole world
seems to be worried about how I'm going to support us."

I put my arm around her. "It isn't like that,
Mom. Molly and I were just talking and . . ."

Mom stood up. "Never mind. I think it's a great
idea. I could mention that I've done clown makeup
and I've also worked for a community theater
group. I'll write the ad after dinner and send it in
first thing in the morning. Even with my job, we
could use some extra cash. And who knows? Maybe
the ad will turn up something really interesting."

If I'd known what that ad was going to turn up,
I'd have stopped her right then.

CHAPTER 3

The next week Molly came home with me after school. She made a big fuss over Corey when we picked him up at school, but he barely spoke to her and ran ahead of us.

"What's with him?" Molly asked. "He's always been my little buddy."

"I don't know. He's been a lot different lately. I don't think he likes the new school." Since Molly and I had moved up to seventh grade this fall, our whole class had switched to the big junior/senior high school. It had been scary at first, but at least we still knew a lot of the kids. Corey had to switch to the elementary school in our new neighborhood. All of his friends were back in his old school.

But that was only part of Corey's problem. I knew he really missed Dad. Even when Dad had started being away a lot, he still managed to do things with Corey. It was a big deal for him to have a son to take to ball games and things. Dad would've taken me too, but I always hated base-ball.

We arrived home and were met by Jaspar's usual greeting. "Go on up to my room, Molly," I said. "I'm going to take the dog out for a few minutes so he'll leave us alone."

It wasn't until I had latched the gate behind me and unhooked Jaspar from his leash that I noticed the old lady digging with a hoe in the back yard. She wasn't any taller than me, and skinny. She wore a long black coat that came almost to her ankles and her hair was fastened in a bun on top of her head. I tried to grab Jaspar's collar, but it was too late. He was heading across the yard like a freight train. The old lady turned around and saw him just before he jumped up on her. As he stood on his hind legs, he was as tall as she was, but he didn't knock her over. She dropped her hoe and grabbed his paws as if he had just asked her to dance. The two of them stumbled around for a few steps.

"Look at this. Look at this," she said.

I finally got close enough to grab Jaspar's collar. "I'm really sorry. He won't hurt you. He's just a little too friendly."

"Of course he won't hurt me. He looks just like my old Barney."

"Really? I didn't think there was another dog in the whole world who looked like Jaspar."

"Ah, Jaspar, is it? I'll have to get some doggie biscuits for you, and a nice bone."

"Do you live around here?" I asked.

She let go of Jaspar's paws and pointed to our house. "I'm Celia Benevenuto. My son Tony just moved me into this house, the back apartment." She made a face. "Moved me from the country to the city in one day."

"You mean Vincent's apartment?" I asked.

She smiled. "Yes, the nice Italian boy with the band. He had to move out in a hurry. Something about not paying the rent, I think. He's storing a few things in my attic until he gets settled."

"That makes us neighbors then. I'm Jenna. My mom, my brother, and I live in the front of the house."

"And Jaspar?"

"Oh sure, Jaspar goes wherever we go. He's family."

"Family. Without my family butting in, I'd be home where I belong." Mrs. Benevenuto picked up her hoe and started hacking away at the grass in the corner of the yard. "How do you grow vegetables in city dirt? The soil in my garden at home was so rich, if I put a broomstick in it, it would sprout. Tony said he'd put fertilizer in here, but what does he know from fertilizer? He never grew a thing in his life. Some city-slicker farmer he is."

"Are you going to make a garden here?" I asked. Out of the corner of my eye, I could see Jaspar zeroing in on his target.

Mrs. Benevenuto hacked away even harder. "My son said, 'I'll dig a garden for you with my bare hands,' but I told him with a shovel it goes faster." She shook her head. "He means well, but he's a busy man. If I want to have a garden ready for next spring, I'll have to dig it myself, even though you can't grow anything in cement like this."

"Why did you move here if you didn't want to?"

"They want to have me close to them, so they can keep an eye on me—my son and his wife." She stopped working and leaned on the hoe. "What kind of a place is this to live in, anyway? You like it here?"

"It's okay. We haven't been here too long, but we like the house, and the yard is nice. Maybe I could help you fix up the garden."

Jaspar finally found his special spot, about two feet from where Mrs. Benevenuto had been hoeing.

She laughed. "Look, Jenna. Jaspar wants to help, too. Already he fertilizes my garden."

* * *

I finally got Jaspar into the house, even though I had to drag him away from a couple of kids who were playing in front of the house next door. Corey was curled up on the couch, watching TV, when I got inside.

"Why don't you turn that thing off and go play outside, Corey? The kids next door look like they're having fun."

"Maybe later," Corey mumbled. "This is my favorite show—Ranger Ralph and Dr. Molar, the Doggie Dentist."

"They're all your favorite show," I yelled over my shoulder as I went up the stairs. "If you can't tear yourself away from the TV, you could at least invite those kids in. You're turning into a hermit."

When I got up to my room, I pulled my homework out of my backpack, but homework wasn't what Molly had on her mind.

"I've found the perfect dress for your mother to wear to open house, Jenna. It's blue, Mr. Bartholomew's favorite color." She settled in on my bed, plumping up the pillows.

"How do you know his favorite color?"

Molly flashed her don't-be-so-dumb-Jenna smile. "Because every day he's worn a blue tie."

"It's the same stupid tie every day, Molly. He

probably only has one. For all you know, he's color blind."

Molly got up. "If we don't stop arguing about dumb things like Mr. Bartholomew's ties, we'll never get the open house plan mapped out before your mother comes home."

"I really don't think that getting my mother married off is going to be the answer to our problems. Besides, if you want to find somebody to support us, why choose a teacher? They don't make all that much money, do they?"

"Use your head, Jenna. Being a teacher is about the hardest job there is. Wouldn't you ask for a ton of money if you had to teach kids like Randy Schloss and Kimberly Stickle?"

"Yeah, I guess you're right."

"Besides, they don't work in the summer, so you can take nice long vacation trips instead of just two weeks."

Corey's piercing wail came up the stairs. "Jenna, come get Jaspar away from the TV." I could hear Jaspar barking in the background.

I yelled down to him. "Just shut him up in the kitchen, Corey. We're busy."

"I can't. He's too big to move, and he's growling."

I turned to Molly. "Come on. I have to get dinner ready before Mom comes home, so we might as well go down and take care of the dog."

Corey was tugging on Jaspar's leash, while the dog snarled at the TV screen. "Jaspar doesn't like Dr. Molar."

Molly grabbed Jaspar's collar. "I know what you mean, Jaspar. I don't like my dentist either. I never tried to bite him, though."

Dr. Molar was a St. Bernard—a talking St. Bernard. He was giving a lecture on why you should floss your teeth. "Jaspar's just jealous because he can't talk like Dr. Molar," Corey said. "Dumb dog."

Molly squinted at the TV screen. "I wonder how they get him to do that?"

"The dog's mouth keeps moving whether he's saying anything or not, Molly. He's a lousy lip-syncher. Come on, let's take Jaspar with us so Corey doesn't miss out on any more hot flossing tips."

We dragged Jaspar into the kitchen and closed both doors. I looked at the note on the refrigerator. It was macaroni and cheese for the third time this week and the usual salad. I handed Molly a head of lettuce and the salad bowl. "Here, you can do this."

Molly started tearing up the lettuce. "Does your mother have a nice pair of heels?"

"I've never noticed. She just has regular-looking feet. What kind of a stupid question is that, anyway?"

Molly rolled her eyes. "Not her feet, silly. Her shoes. Does she have some nice heels that would go with a sapphire blue dress?"

"Did anyone ever tell you you have a one-track mind? Just forget this whole plan, Molly, because there's no way Mom's going to . . ."

Just then Jaspar threw himself against the door that led to the front hall, barking furiously. Mom opened the door a crack and peeked through. "Why is Jaspar shut up in here?"

"He and Corey couldn't agree on which channel to watch."

Mom smiled and settled down at the table to sort through the mail. "I see. Just another normal day around here, I gather. Hi, Molly. How's your family?" She studied Molly's face intently.

"Fine, thanks, Mrs. Bryant. Mom said to say hello." Mom had her head tilted to one side and was squinting at Molly now.

"Is there something wrong with my face, Mrs. Bryant?" Molly asked, leaning toward Mom.

Mom laughed and rubbed her hand over her eyes. "I'm sorry, Molly. Staring at faces is a carry-over from my new job, I guess. Did Jenna tell you what I'm doing?"

Who would tell anyone their mother was a zit zapper?

"No, she didn't, Mrs. Bryant."

"Well, I'm working at the school picture plant as a spotter. We're the ones who fill in the white spots that are left when they take the pimples off the negatives. We're called zit zappers."

"Really? Hey, that's great. You find the most fascinating jobs, Mrs. Bryant. Not dull stuff like my mom."

"Well, the only trouble is I can't look at anybody's face now without mentally zapping their zits."

Molly ran to the hall mirror. "I have a zit?"

"Relax, Molly," I said. "Mom was just fascinated by your freckles. Your face would keep her busy for a week."

Molly was going to make a nasty remark, but the phone rang and Mom picked it up.

"Yes, I did . . . Certainly I'd be interested . . . Well, yes. I have some pictures of my children . . . Fine, I'll bring them in tomorrow."

Mom was beaming when she hung up. "You'll never guess who that was."

"The head zit zapper wants you to bring in pictures of Jenna and Corey for the new zappers to practice on," Molly volunteered.

Mom walked across the kitchen in a daze, as if she'd just been struck by lightning. "I can't believe it. The people at one of the local TV stations want to make up the whole news team for Halloween.

They have a makeup person, but she doesn't do anything out of the ordinary. I'm supposed to bring over examples of my makeup tomorrow after work. If they like what they see, they're willing to pay me a hundred dollars."

"TV?" Molly squeaked. "That's really terrific, Mrs. Bryant. I told you, you find the neatest jobs."

"You sure this isn't some kind of a joke?" I asked. "Which channel?"

"WAKY, Channel Seven," Mom said. "It's just over on Alberta Street. That's only three blocks away, and it's close to Class Memories, so I'll go right there from work. I wonder where I packed the clown and stage makeup?" She started rummaging through a carton in the dining room. "Jenna, see if you can find some Halloween pictures of you and Corey from the past few years. Here, they should be in this shoe box."

I took it back to the kitchen table, and Molly and I started going through the snapshots. There was one of Mom, Dad, and me when I was just a baby. Dad was holding me, and the way they were smiling at each other, you could tell they were in love. I found another one of all four of us, taken just last year. In this one Mom and Dad had "say cheese" smiles on their faces and the love-look was gone. I shuffled through some more snapshots, looking for clues that would show when they fell out of love,

but I couldn't find any. I had lived right there in
the same house with Mom and Dad and never realized something terrible was happening to them
until it was too late. Maybe if I could have found
some pictures to line up in order from "in love" to
"out of love," the whole thing would have made
some sense.

CHAPTER 4

Halloween came before we knew it. Mom got the job at the TV station. They weren't sure they should use a "nonprofessional," but she showed them pictures of Corey and me in all kinds of Halloween makeup, of herself as a clown, and a group of shots of some of the actors she had made up in the theater group. Pretty soon she had them convinced. She got to use the costumes they had in their wardrobe department, and they even gave her money to get some extra makeup she needed for special effects. She was going right to the TV station from work, so I was supposed to hand out the goodies until she got back.

In the old days Dad went out with us while Mom dressed up as something weird and stayed home to pass out candy. One year she hung a stuffed witch on a broomstick on the front porch. She attached one end of a piece of string to the broomstick and held the other end, hiding behind a curtain. Each time someone came to the house, she pulled on the string, and the witch slowly swung around, as if watching the trick-or-treaters come up the side-walk. Even though we knew how it worked, it still gave me the creeps when we got home. Dad used to laugh and say Mom was a kid at heart.

"Come on, Corey. I'll get you into your costume now, so you'll be all ready for your makeup when Mom gets home."

"I don't want to go out this year."

"You have to go out. Mom stayed up half the night finishing this for you." I held up the costume. It was a green dinosaur with big orange scales sticking out from the neck to the end of the stuffed tail. She'd made it out of an old green blanket and an orange felt pumpkin costume I used to have. She just dreamed it up out of her head without using a pattern.

"I changed my mind. I want to be something scary. Dinosaurs aren't scary."

The doorbell rang. It was a tiny Snow White with an older girl who was supposed to be a gypsy. I held out the candy dish and the big girl took just one, but Snow White grabbed a whole handful. "Knock it off, Snow," I said. "Leave some for the dwarfs." Snow White stuck her tongue out at me, and I closed the door in her face. I could see that trick-or-treating was a lot more fun when you were on the other side of the door.

Corey had put the dinosaur hood on Jaspar, and he looked like a prehistoric pet. "See, Corey? Jaspar looks scary as a dinosaur."

"He looks dumb, not scary."

I had to figure out a way to get Corey into his costume. Mom would be heartbroken if he didn't wear it. I decided to distract him. "The news must have already started. Let's watch the people Mom did the makeup for. Look, Corey. There they are." The anchorwoman had a skeleton's face and hands and wore a sheer gray robe with a hood. The sportscaster was Frankenstein, with screws sticking out of his neck and a realistic-looking scar across his forehead. They both looked great, but they were just talking in their normal voices and seemed embarrassed.

Then it was time for the weather, and Dracula swept onto the screen. "I vant to tell you about the veather," he said. "It vill be vindy tonight, but on Vednesday it vill be even vorse." He threw back his head and gave a blood-curdling cackle, revealing two long fangs. "There's a varm front creeping in from the vest," he said, drawing his long purple fingernail across a map of the country, "oozing across Visconsin and dripping down into Vest Virginia like blood." Another cackle.

Jaspar put his head down between his paws and whimpered. The big orange scale on top of his dino hood fell over one eye. Just then Mom came through the door. "Have you seen them? How do they look?"

"Great, Mom," I said. "The weatherman is getting a little carried away, though."

Mom smiled. "That's Wayne Weston. He's a real nut. The whole makeup thing was his idea."

We watched as he finished his report. "This is Vayne Veston, TV Seven's veird veatherman varning you if you vander outside tonight, vatch for vinged creatures. It's vonderful veather for... bats!"

"Veird isn't the vord," I said. "That guy's missing a few screws."

"Yes, he is," Mom said. "I borrowed them for Frankenstein's neck. Hey, why aren't you two in your costumes?"

"I'm too old this year, Mom. I'll just take Corey around." Actually I would have gone out with Molly if we were back in our old neighborhood. I just felt funny about doing it here.

"You sure? You can wear my clown costume, or I think I have an old witch hat packed in one of those cartons in the corner of the dining room."

"I'm really past the costume stage, Mom. I can't seem to get in the mood this year."

Mom looked sad for a minute, then came over and raised my chin with her fingertips. "I could whip up a great face for you in no time." She grinned and tossed her hair over one shoulder. "I'm a professional, you know. I do TV stars."

I hugged her. "Yeah, I heard, but I'll pass. Get Corey ready and we'll go out, okay?" I hoped Corey had forgotten about not wanting to be a dinosaur. He hadn't.

"I don't like my costume," he said, folding his arms firmly. "I'm not putting it on."

"I thought you wanted to be a dinosaur," Mom said, taking off her coat. "Every kid in the world wants to be a dinosaur."

"Not me. I want to be something big and scary."

Mom thought for a minute, then leaned toward Corey, her eyes wide. "Do you know the biggest, scariest thing I can think of?"

"The scariest thing? What?" Corey asked. He had that little catch in his voice that he gets when Mom tells ghost stories.

"A fire-breathing dragon."

"Yes, yes! That's what I want to be. A fire-breezing dragon."

Mom pulled out her makeup kit and started painting red and orange flames that flickered out of the corners of Corey's mouth and flared out over his cheeks. Then she added purple smoke that curled up over his eyebrows and into his hair.

Corey could barely sit still. "I want to see." He pushed a chair over to the hall mirror. "That's scary," he squeaked. "That's what I wanted to be all along."

Mom picked up the dinosaur costume, flourishing it like a bullfighter's cape. "And here's you fire-breathing dragon's body."

"A dragon's body. I'll be big and scary." Corey climbed into the suit, and Mom adjusted the stuffed feet so that the orange stuffed claws curled down over his sneakers.

"Now for the finishing touch," Mom said, whisking the hood away from Jaspar. "Your big, scary, fire-breathing dragon's head."

Corey grabbed it before she could put it on his head. "That's not a fire-breezing dragon's head. That's a dumb old dinosaur head. Dragons need long snouts for the fire to come out of."

Mom started to say something; then she handed the hood to me and ran for the stairs. "You're right, Corey. One snout, coming up."

In a flash she was back with her sewing basket. She sat on the couch and snipped off the big scale on the dino hood. Then she started pinning it around the top of the face opening. I sat next to her and leaned close so Corey wouldn't hear. "If you pull this off, you deserve a medal."

"Mmmnrff," Mom said, her mouth bristling with
pins. She always held the pins like that when she
sewed, and it drove me nuts. She threaded a nee-
dle and started sewing the scale in place. I wasn't
sure what she was trying to make, but it didn't look
like a dragon. "There," Mom said, biting off the
end of the thread. That was another thing that
drove me crazy. Mom couldn't even sew like a normal person. She took two round yellow buttons and
sewed them on top of the hood. Then she popped
it on Corey's head. I couldn't believe it. The orange
scale curved around Corey's forehead and stuck out
like a snout, with the flames and smoke billowing
out from underneath.

Corey seemed to grow six inches as she fastened
the hood under his chin. "Hold still," Mom said, as
she made a dot with a black marker in each of the
buttons.

"Hey, they're eyes," I said. "Not bad, Mom."

"I want to see," Corey squeaked. He ran to the
hall mirror again, his heavy tail almost knocking
over a lamp.

"Watch out, all you people out there," he said to
the mirror. "A big old scary old fire-breezing
dragon is coming to get you. Hurry up, Jenna."

I grabbed my jacket and followed him out the
door. "Hold on. You forgot your bag and your flashlight."

"Dragons can see in the dark."

"Maybe so," I said, shoving the flashlight into his hand, "but this is so other people can see *you*."

I could hear small groups of kids farther down the street, but there was nobody in sight. We stopped in front of the first house. "You want me to go to the door with you?"

I could see the flashlight trembling in Corey's hand, but he stuck out his chin. "No. Dragons do things all by themselves." He went up and rang the doorbell and even yelled "trick or treat" when a lady opened the door.

"Next time, remember to say thank you," I said, as he ran back to me. "Even dragons are supposed to be polite."

"Okay," Corey mumbled, shining the flashlight inside the bag to see what he got. "A candy bar. Neat-o!" The next house didn't have any lights on, so we didn't stop there. Corey half-skipped down the sidewalk, his tail gathering up dry leaves as it zigzagged along with a scritching sound.

I could see flashlight beams bobbing their way up the street toward us, and when we stopped at the fourth house, we met a man with two little kids—a clown and a robot. The man stayed back on the sidewalk with me while the three kids ran up to ring the bell. All of a sudden I felt like an old lady—like I was thirty or something.

"Nice night, isn't it?" the man remarked.

It was nice. An almost-full moon was peeking through deep purple clouds with white edges. "Yeah, great," I said, then looked at him. At first I thought he was really ugly, but then I realized he was wearing one of those phony noses with big glasses and a mustache attached.

The lady in the doorway put something into the other kids' bags and got to Corey last. As she gave him his candy, she looked over his shoulder and saw the man standing next to me. "Oh, look at your father. Isn't that a funny mask?"

Corey turned around suddenly, his eyes wide under the snout. "Daddy?" he called, as he started running back down the walk.

"Corey, watch out," I yelled, but it was too late. His feet had already tangled in the big tail and he sprawled out on the sidewalk, candy flying in all directions.

The man got to him before I did and picked him up. "Hey, little guy, take it easy."

Corey was crying and smiling at the same time as he reached up to pull off the man's glasses. Then he started beating against the man's chest. "Put me down. You're not my daddy. Let me go."

"Hey, I was just trying to help." The man set Corey down next to me and grabbed his kids' hands.

Corey pulled my sleeve. "I want to go home now," he wailed.

"Wait a minute. Don't you want to pick up the candy you dropped?"

"I don't care about any old candy. I just want to go home." He took off, running.

I ran to catch up and grabbed the end of his tail. "Look, just because you thought that man was Dad doesn't mean you have to . . ."

Corey wasn't listening. He reached our front sidewalk and scrambled up the porch steps. As he burst through the front door, a huge figure met us. It raised its arms, and a purple-lined black cape filled the whole hall.

"The monster from the wall got out!" Corey screamed as he slammed into my stomach and tried to burrow right through me.

I looked up into a white face with black lips and two long fangs. "I vant to drink your bloooooood," it howled, then let loose with a cackle.

Corey shrieked and shoved me back out of the house. I would have run too, but the cackle sounded familiar. It was the idiot from the TV station.

Mom heard Corey's screams and came rushing out from the kitchen. "What happened? Is Corey hurt?" she said, as she ran outdoors.

"I'm sorry," Wayne Weston answered, waving his

purple-nailed hands around helplessly. "I didn't
mean to scare him. I was just kidding around."

Corey dove for Mom and clung to her leg, sobbing. Mom pried him loose and brought him back
into the house. She sat in the big wingback chair,
cradling him in her arms. He kept right on crying,
barely stopping to take a breath. "It's just the man
from the TV station, honey. One of the people
Mommy did the makeup for, remember?"

"What are you doing here?" I asked. "I thought
Mom did the makeup at the station."

"She did, but I have this habit of rubbing my
eyes when I think, and I smeared my eye makeup
all over my face. I called your mother, and she said
to come over and she'd fix it up for the eleven
o'clock news."

How stupid could you get, rubbing your eyes
with makeup on? Even Corey knew enough not to
do that. And who did he think he was, trying to
scare us like that? I just glared at Wayne. He
turned away and went over to Corey. "Look,
Corey, I'm not really Dracula, see? It's just a costume."

Corey raised his head to look at him and started
screaming again. "I don't think this is going to
work, Wayne," Mom said. "It's not as if you had on
a mask that you could take off. You really do look
frightening. I think you'd better leave. I was fin-

ished touching up the makeup anyway."

Wayne stopped where I was waiting by the front door. "I'm sorry, really. I never meant to scare you and Corey."

Corey was still sobbing into Mom's chest, his orange scales quivering, his snout with the buggy yellow eyes peering over her shoulder.

I looked Dracula right in the eye. "You didn't scare *me*," I said.

CHAPTER 5

Corey was too upset to go to school the next day, so
Mom had to stay home with him. He was on the
couch watching TV when I came home. Mom was
in the dining room unpacking some of the cartons
that had been there since we moved. She had little
piles of stuff all over the living room furniture.

"How's Corey?" I asked. "Has he gotten over
being scared half to death yet?"

Mom put her finger up to her lips and pulled me
into the kitchen. "He won't talk about it, just says
he has a stomachache from all the candy he ate. I
know Wayne looked pretty frightening, but I can't
understand why it's taking Corey this long to get
over it."

I dropped my books on the kitchen table. "That
guy didn't just *look* frightening, Mom. He made a
big deal out of scaring us with his 'I vant to drink

your blooooood' act." I held out my jacket in an imitation of Wayne's cape.

Mom shushed me again. "I'm sure Wayne didn't mean it. He was having such fun with the costume and makeup, he just didn't think."

"Well, grown-ups are supposed to think before they do something stupid. Besides, if Corey has a stomachache, it isn't from candy because he never got to eat any. He spilled his treats all over the sidewalk when he fell."

"You didn't tell me he fell. Was he hurt?"

"Not physically."

Mom jammed her hands into her pockets, the gesture she always used when she was getting annoyed with me. "What's that supposed to mean, Jenna?"

I told her about Corey thinking the man with the big nose was Dad.

"Oh no," Mom moaned, as she dropped into a kitchen chair. "Then he ran home to find Dracula in the front hall, the poor baby. Why didn't you tell me about this before?"

"Things were so crazy after we got home, it slipped my mind. I'm not used to being greeted by monsters, you know."

Just then the doorbell rang. "Get that, will you, Jenna? I want to talk to Corey. And if somebody's selling something, we don't want any."

There was a man at the door, holding a bouquet of flowers. His ears stuck out like the handles on a sugar bowl, and his jacket was so tight across his stomach, the buttons were straining to hold it together.

"If you're selling flowers, we don't want any," I said.

"No, I'm not selling these." A gust of wind blew the hair away from a bald spot on the top of his head. He raked his fingers through it, trying to put it back into place. "I brought them for your mother —a sort of peace offering." There was something familiar about the voice, but before I could place it, Mom was behind me, reaching out for the flowers.

"Wayne, what a nice surprise. You didn't have to do this. Come on in. Have you met my daughter Jenna? This is Wayne Weston from the TV station."

"We met briefly, but I think we could use a new start." He held out his hand. "Glad to meet you, Jenna."

A new start for what? Why did he have to come back, anyway? I just stared at him while he pumped my hand up and down.

Mom came over with Corey. "This is Wayne Weston, Corey. He's the weatherman on television." Corey wasn't interested at first, but he brightened at the word "television."

"Really?" Corey asked, dragging Wayne over to the couch. "Do you know Ranger Ralph?" He knocked some books on the floor to make room for Wayne to sit down.

"Sure. I know him real well. Want to come over to the station to meet him sometime?"

Corey bounced up and down on the cushion. "Could I, Mom? Please? Could we meet Dr. Molar, too?"

"You know who this is, Corey?" I asked, glaring at Wayne.

Mom put her hand on my shoulder. "Jenna, I wouldn't . . ."

I shook her hand away. "It's Dracula. The one who scared the pants off you last night." There, let Wayne try to weasel his way out of that.

Corey looked at Wayne, then back at me. "Is not."

"I'm afraid Jenna's right, Corey," Wayne said. He reached in his pocket and pulled out a set of white plastic fangs. "It was just a Halloween costume, like yours." He slipped the fangs over his teeth and clicked them a few times. "See?"

Wayne didn't look a bit scary sitting there with his big ears and his fangs. He just looked dumb.

"That wasn't you," Corey said, ducking his head

and looking up from under a fringe of bangs.

Wayne reached out and tickled Corey's stomach.
"I vant to drink your bloooood."

Corey giggled. "It *was* you, wasn't it?"

"Yessss. It vas me. I didn't mean to scare you,
though."

Corey stood up and stuck out his chest. "I wasn't
scared. I was a big scary fire-breezing dragon, and
dragons aren't afraid of anybody. I was only pre-
tending to be scared."

Wayne grinned. "You're about the best actor I
ever saw, Corey. Anyone who acts as well as you
ought to have his own TV show when he grows up.
How about the Captain Corey Show?"

"And Jaspar could be Dr. Molar," Corey
shouted, completely won over. I couldn't believe
it.

Mom sniffed her flowers. "Mmm. I should get
these in water. Could I get you a cup of coffee,
Wayne?"

Wayne looked at his watch. "Thanks just the
same, but I'm on my dinner hour from work, and I
wondered if I could take you all out to eat. I have
an idea I'd like to talk over with you, Lois."

Corey pulled at Mom's sleeve. "Could we eat
Chinese? Could we go to the Pagoda? Please?" His
stomach had suddenly recovered.

Wayne shrugged and looked at Mom. "That okay with you?"

"Sounds great."

"The Pagoda it is, then," Wayne said, hefting his bulk up off the couch.

Corey was already in his jacket. I swear he'd go off with Atilla the Hun if Atilla offered him an egg roll.

Wayne drove us over to the Pagoda in his beat-up old car. We used to go there all the time when we lived in our old house. Dad loved Chinese food. Now it was only a few blocks from where we lived, but there was never any extra money to go out and eat. There was barely enough money to eat at all, for pete's sake. I was getting pretty sick of macaroni. When we got to the restaurant, Corey led us over to our old table and even had Wayne sit in Dad's seat.

Wayne opened the menu. "What does everybody want?"

"Egg rolls," Corey said. "About a hundred million of them."

Mom reached over to pull off his jacket. "Why don't you start with one."

"That sounds like a good idea," Wayne said. "Then, if you're still hungry, we'll order the other ninety-nine million nine hundred and ninety-nine."

Corey and Mom laughed as if that had been the greatest joke in the world. I didn't. I just scrunched down behind my menu and pretended Dad was sitting across from me in his old seat. I stuffed some crunchy Chinese noodles into my mouth so I wouldn't have to say anything.

"Why don't you do the ordering, Wayne," Mom said. "All Corey eats are egg rolls, and Jenna and I are adventurous. We'll try anything."

I peeked over my menu at her. She was smiling all over the place and pouring Wayne a cup of tea. When the waiter came, Wayne ordered some stuff I never heard of, then excused himself to go call the TV station about something.

"Why didn't you order shrimp with lobster sauce?" I asked. "That's your favorite thing in the whole world, isn't it?"

Mom smiled and shrugged. "I just thought it would be better to let Wayne make the choice. When you're older and start dating, Jenna, you'll learn that it's better to let the boy make the choice until you get to know him. Otherwise you might order something that's too expensive."

"Dating!" I said, loud enough for the people at the next table to hear. "Is that what this is? A *date*?"

We could see Wayne working his way back across

the dining room. Mom leaned close to me, whispering. "No, this is not a date, and I want you to start behaving yourself. We probably will never see this man again, but it's very nice of him to treat us to dinner to make up for last night."

Mom gave me her "you're on thin ice" look as Wayne reached our table. "There, that should give me a little more time for dinner," he said. "The low temperature reports are coming in from our weather spotters in the outlying areas, and I just wanted to make sure someone was there to record them."

"Being a TV weatherman must be fun," Mom said. She sounded like a cheerleader on her first date with the high school football star, for pete's sake. It was sickening.

Wayne spread both hands out on the table. "That's what I wanted to talk to you about. Reporting the weather is a pretty dull business in Rochester. There are just so many ways to say 'cloudy,' and we never get any really exciting weather. You know—life-threatening storms. We haven't even had much in the way of winter snowstorms in the past few years. Up until now it's been almost boring."

"Up until now?" Mom asked, leaning back so the waiter could put our dinner on the table.

"Until last night—the Dracula bit. I loved it, and"—he leaned closer to Mom, wiggling his eyebrows—"so did the station manager. I convinced him that we could improve our rating on the news show by putting some fun into the weather. That's where you come in."

"How?" Mom asked. "Are you going to be Dracula from now on?"

"No, I'm going to be a 'weather personality'— Weird Wayne Weston, WAKY's Wacky Weatherman. I can be all different things, depending on the season. The possibilities are endless—Jack Frost, one of Santa's reindeer, a Thanksgiving turkey."

"That one ought to be easy," I mumbled into a mound of Chinese vegetables that had been put in front of me.

"That sounds great," Mom said, "but it would involve more than just makeup. You're talking about some pretty complicated costumes here, and I didn't see anything like that in your wardrobe department."

"That's just it. We need someone who can put together the costumes as well as do makeup, and from what we saw in those pictures you brought to the station, you're the one for the job. They want to do a trial period, maybe for the next month, with a new costume each week." Wayne rubbed his hands together. "What do you think? Interested?"

Mom shrugged and smiled. "Sure. I guess I could manage that on top of my regular job. It sounds as if it might be fun."

"You could use my dragon costume sometime," Corey said, slathering his egg roll with hot mustard.

He started to pick it up, and Wayne reached out to stop him. "Whoa, little buddy. You'd better take it easy on that mustard. It's pretty hot stuff."

Corey ignored him and took a huge bite. "I like it this way," he said with his mouth full.

Wayne shook his head. "Now I know why you make such a great fire-breathing dragon. You have asbestos lips."

Corey nodded, licking the mustard off his mouth. "I have the bestest lips of anybody in my whole school."

Mom and Wayne had a big laugh over that. As if that weren't enough, Wayne asked, "What do you get if a hen lays an egg on a hill? How about you, Jenna? Want to take a guess?"

I took a mouthful of vegetables and shook my head.

Wayne looked around the table, grinning. "Give up?" He slapped his hand down on the table, making our tea cups clatter. "You get an egg roll!"

The way Mom and Corey were laughing, you would've thought he was Bill Cosby.

Wayne's eyes were all watery from laughing. "Here's another one. If a barn faces to the east and a rooster lays an egg on the peak of the barn roof, which side of the roof will the egg roll down? Will it go toward the north or the south?"

Other people were starting to notice our table. It was like trying to eat in the middle of a game show.

"Give up?" Wayne asked not only us but the people at the next three tables, too.

Everybody gave up.

"It's not going to roll down either side," he crowed, "because a rooster can't lay an egg!"

Half of the restaurant laughed, and a few people groaned. The whole rest of the meal went like that, with Wayne telling terrible jokes and everybody but me laughing. I'd never been so embarrassed in my whole life.

Finally it was over, and the waiter brought a little tray with four fortune cookies on it. Wayne held the tray out to me. "Here, Jenna, you choose the first one. That way the fortune will really be meant for you instead of just a leftover from somebody else."

I looked at him, sitting there in Dad's seat as if he thought he belonged there. I cracked open the brittle cookie and slipped out a thin blue strip of paper. It read: "Beware of Strangers Bearing Gifts."

That was exactly what I intended to do.

CHAPTER 6

Mom left a note on the refrigerator the next day, telling me not to start supper. Corey glued himself to the TV as soon as we got in the house, so I went up to my room and did my math and English homework. Just when my stomach was starting to growl, and I was thinking about going downstairs to get a snack, I heard Mom come in.

"Hi, Mom," I said, meeting her in the kitchen. "What's with dinner? You planning something special?"

"I sure am," she said, pulling a steak from her grocery bag. "This look special enough to you?"

"Steak? Are you kidding? We haven't had steak in months. What's the occasion? Did I forget somebody's birthday?"

"No, that's your father's trick," she said, slipping a carton of ice cream into the freezer.

She was talking about my birthday last summer

when Dad forgot to call or send a present until a
week later. "That wasn't Dad's fault. You know that
Gladys dragged him off to Las Vegas that weekend.
She made him forget."

"Ah, yes," Mom said, slamming a cupboard shut.
"Beautiful blonde Gladys, the Vanna White of the
recreational vehicle industry."

Mom always got touchy when I mentioned
Gladys. I wished she'd just forget about the birthday incident, though. Dad remembered it as soon
as he got home, and he felt really bad. Anyway, it
was *my* birthday he forgot, not Mom's.

"Do you think you could hold off on eating until
a little later, Jenna? About seven?"

"Arghh!" I clutched my stomach and staggered
around the kitchen, doing my dying-of-starvation
act.

Mom laughed. "Okay, okay, I get the idea. You
and Corey can eat right away."

"What about you?"

"I'll eat later with Wayne. He can't get here until
after he does the six o'clock news." She turned her
back to me and started cutting up onions.

"Why is Wayne coming here?"

"We need to talk about his costumes and
makeup. Besides, I wanted to invite him to dinner
to thank him."

"Thank him for what?"

Mom made a sudden dash for the sink, turned on the faucet full blast, then bent over and stared into the stream of water. She always did that when her eyes watered from cutting onions. It looked stupid, but she claimed it made her eyes stop burning. "To thank him for taking us out to dinner last night," she said, her words echoing in the stainless steel sink.

"But he took us out in the first place to make up for scaring Corey. If you invite him here to dinner to thank him for *that* dinner, then he'll invite us out to dinner to thank you for *this* dinner. Then you'll have him over for dinner to thank him for thanking us. We're going to be stuck having dinner with Wayne Weston for the rest of our lives!"

Mom stood up and blotted her eyes with a paper towel. "That sounds just fine to me. Call your brother and tell him it's time to eat."

The steak was good, but I could hardly swallow it. I knew Mom wasn't kidding when she said she wouldn't mind having Wayne around all the time, and she didn't seem to care whether I wanted him around or not. She didn't even sit with us while we ate. She ran upstairs to "get ready," and a few minutes later I could hear her singing in the shower. After Corey and I finished eating, I cleared up our dishes and stuck them in the sink. I wanted to get out of the way before Wayne arrived, but I wasn't fast enough.

"Jenna!" Mom called down the stairs. "I heard the doorbell. Will you answer it and entertain Wayne until I get down there?"

"Let me! I want to open the door for Wayne," Corey yelled, pushing past me. He swung the door open and threw his hands over his head. "I vant to drink your bloooood!" he shrieked and collapsed in a fit of giggles on the floor.

"Not bad, Corey," Wayne said. "Not bad. You'll be on TV yet."

Corey jumped up and pushed Wayne toward the couch. "Did you say hello to Ranger Ralph and Dr. Molar for me?"

I couldn't figure Corey out. Two days ago, he'd cried himself soggy because the man in the nose and mustache wasn't Dad. Then he got hysterical when Wayne met him at the door. Now he was making a big fuss over Wayne and had forgotten all about Dad.

Wayne eased himself down on the couch and reached into his pocket. "Glad you reminded me. Ranger Ralph sent this to you."

Corey climbed into his lap. "Jenna, look what Wayne brought for me. A picture of Ranger Ralph and Dr. Molar!"

Wayne pointed to the bottom of the picture. "It's autographed, see?"

Corey wrinkled up his nose. "What's otto-grabbed?" He handed me the picture.

"It means Ranger Ralph signed it," I said.

"He even wrote your name on it," Wayne added. "Doctor Molar put his paw print on it, too."

"Wait till I show the kids in my class," Corey squealed. "They all watch Ranger Ralph."

I suddenly realized the picture was soggy on one side. "Why is this wet?"

Wayne made his face droop, so he looked just like a St. Bernard. "Dr. Molar has this little problem. He drools."

"Gross!" I handed the picture back to Corey and wiped my hand on my jeans.

Just then Mom swept down the stairs and into the room. I mean really *swept*, like one of those old-time movie stars. She wasn't wearing a long gown or anything—just jeans and her fuzzy purple sweater—but she looked like Cinderella at the ball. Her hair was freshly washed and shiny, and she smelled wonderful. Wayne jumped up when she came into the room, patting his hair into place over the bald spot. I could tell Mom was about to go into her lovesick cheerleader act again. I couldn't stand to watch, so I went back upstairs.

Even with my door closed I could hear all the

laughing going on in the living room. Then I smelled steak and onions cooking, and the noise was coming from the kitchen. I was glad Corey was down there, so Wayne couldn't try to get fresh with Mom. She probably wouldn't know how to handle a situation like that anymore. She and Dad had been married for almost fifteen years. You could forget an awful lot about dating in that length of time.

I fell asleep with my social studies book propped on my stomach and woke up when I heard footsteps in the hall. It was a few minutes after nine o'clock. I peeked out and saw Mom in Corey's room, tucking him into bed.

She noticed me when she heard my door creak. "Wayne had us laughing, and we forgot the time," she said. "Corey should have been in bed an hour ago. You'd better start settling in too, Jenna."

"Okay, Mom. Did Wayne just leave?"

She stopped at the top of the stairs to give me a hug. "No, he's still here, honey. We have a lot to talk about." She smiled and kissed me on the forehead, then hippity-hopped down the stairs like a teenager.

I listened for laughter, but I didn't hear any. I could just imagine what was going on now. I slipped into the hall and crept down the stairs to where I could see into the living room. They were on the couch with their backs to me, leaning close together and speaking in hushed voices. Every now and then Mom giggled.

I'd been right about Wayne. He was definitely moving in on Mom, and I had to think of some way to stop him. Molly! She'd know what to do, but it was too late. Our mothers had given us strict orders not to call each other after nine o'clock, even in an emergency.

If Dad knew about Wayne, he'd put a stop to it, fast. He'd probably come right home to try to talk some sense into Mom. When he saw her, he might even realize what a terrible mistake he'd made by leaving her to marry Gladys. And he'd remember how much he missed Corey . . . and me.

That was it! How could I have been so stupid? All I had to do was call Dad and talk to him about how things were. Not one of those family calls where all I got from Mom was "Here, say hello to Jenna," but a real heart-to-heart like Dad and I used to have.

I tiptoed into Mom's room and pulled the door shut very slowly, so you could barely hear the click when it latched. My hands were shaking as I flipped through the pages of Mom's address book. I found the number, but it took three times before I could dial it right. I could hear my heart pounding inside the phone as I listened for the first ring.

"Hello." He picked it up on the third ring.

Tears sprang to my eyes as soon as I heard his voice. "Daddy?"

"Jenna? What's wrong, baby? Did something happen to your mother?"

"No. She's fine. I just wanted to talk to you."

"Does she know you're calling?"

"Sure, Daddy."

"Good. Put her on, will you?"

"She's not here right now."

"Not there! It has to be nighttime out there, doesn't it? She hasn't gone off and left you and Corey alone at night, has she?"

"No, she just can't come to the phone right now. Besides, I wanted to talk to you . . . like we used to." My voice cracked.

"Sure, baby. What about?" I heard Gladys in the background, asking who was calling. Dad must have muffled his answer by putting his hand over the receiver.

"I miss you, Daddy. Are you coming back to visit soon?"

"Not for a while, baby. Gladys and I have to go around to the recreational vehicle shows. We're booked for the whole West Coast circuit in the next few months."

I wound the fingers of my free hand in the coils

of the phone cord. "You get some time off, don't you? Couldn't you come then?"

"We've got a show every week, Jenna. Sales have been way down this year. I can't take a chance on missing out. You know how it is."

I didn't know how it was at all. "How about if I came out there, Daddy? You could take me along with you. I could help."

"You'd be bored stiff, baby. Besides, I wouldn't have any time to be with you. I have to hustle every minute I'm there. Gladys is working too, as a model demonstrator."

"Am I ever going to see you again, Daddy?" The lump in my throat was getting so big, I thought it would burst.

Dad's voice got quiet. "Sure, baby. Just as soon as the RV show season slows down in the spring, Gladys and I will drive out there in the brand-new deluxe-model camper that sleeps eight. We'll take you and Corey up to Darien Lake and have a great old time."

"But Daddy, Darien Lake doesn't open up until Memorial Day. That's months from now."

"Well, I'm just talking about our big trip. We'll try to slip in a short visit before then. Maybe Christmas."

"Really? You promise?"

"I can't nail anything down right now, baby, but I'll be calling for sure on Thanksgiving, and we'll set it up then."

"That's great, Daddy, but I think you should come out here sooner."

"I told you, Jenna. I just can't go running..."

I took the plunge. "Mom has a new friend...a man."

There was a pause on the other end of the line. I knew that would get him. At first I thought he was starting to cry. Then I realized he was laughing. "Lois went and got herself a boyfriend? Well, I'll be...! Good for her. You tell her I said that. Good for her."

"But, Daddy..."

"That's wonderful news, Jenna. Your mother's young, and she deserves to kick up her heels a little. I'm very happy for her. Now listen, baby, I've got to go. I'll call you on Thanksgiving, okay? Love you, Babe."

I tried to tell him I loved him too, but the lump in my throat exploded into a sob. By the time I could get the words out, I was talking to a dial tone.

CHAPTER 7

Gym was the first class I had with Molly the next day. She'd been out sick since Halloween, and I hadn't even had a chance to talk to her on the phone. I missed seeing her in the locker room, but I was gaining on her as she rounded the far side of the track on the athletic field. I had to tell her about Mom and Weird Wayne.

"Only Ms. Raskin would make us run outside in November," Molly said, her words coming out in little puffs of steam. "She should be running a gym class for polar bears. This is going to turn my cold into pneumonia."

I grabbed her arm. "Slow down a little. We're far enough away so she can't tell we're talking. Something terrible has happened."

"Again? What now?"

I told her about Wayne scaring Corey on Halloween and how he was hanging around our house all the time now.

Molly's eyes widened. "You're kidding? She's dating him? Even after he scared the pants off Corey on Halloween?"

"Well, she says they're not dating, but I saw them sitting together on the couch last night, and it sure looked like a date to me. Besides, she's going to be spending a lot of time with him. It all started the night before last when he came over to apologize. He brought flowers for Mom and took us all out to dinner."

"This guy doesn't sound too bad, Jenna. At least he apologized. Maybe your mom will solve the husband problem without our help."

"You don't understand, Molly. There's no way I'd want him for a father. He's funny-looking, and he tells these rotten jokes all the time. Now he's going to be WAKY's Wacky Weatherman and make a fool of himself every night on the news. Mom is going to do his costumes and makeup. She says he's coming over again tonight to help her think up ideas."

"Tonight? What about open house?"

"He's coming over after we get home."

"That's bad. If your mom and Mr. Bartholomew really like each other, she can't ask him over to the house if the geek is going to be there."

We were almost back to the starting line, and Ms. Raskin was leaning out into the track with her trusty stopwatch. "Pick up the pace, Welter and Bryant. You're lagging way behind."

Molly sprinted on ahead of me, then slowed down on the far side of the track. "We're going to have to stop meeting like this," I gasped as I finally caught up with her. "You trying out for the Olympics or something?"

"Sorry. I thought I'd better make it look good for a minute or two. Besides, running helps me think. If your mom is getting serious with this Weird Wayne character, it's even more important to get her together with Mr. Bartholomew tonight. I snuck the dress and a pair of shoes to match out of my mother's closet. They're in my locker. Have you said anything to your mother about open house?"

We heard footsteps crunching on the cinders behind us. I looked over my shoulder and saw Kimberly Stickle and a couple of her snooty friends gaining on us. "Well, if it isn't Jenna Bryant, daughter of a real honest-to-goodness zit zapper," Kimberly crowed. "You'll never see an unsightly blemish on her face." They all laughed as they passed us.

"Your whole face is an unsightly blemish, Kimberly," Molly yelled at her back.

"You told!" I whispered to Molly. "Some best friend you are."

"I didn't. I never even speak to that witch. You know that."

"So how did she find out? You're the only person in the whole world who knew about Mom being a zit zapper."

"I don't know. Some of the other kids' mothers probably work at the picture plant this time of year. They hire a lot of extra people from now until Christmas. Any one of them could have told their kid, and Kimberly hasn't missed overhearing a conversation since school started. Now, did you talk to your mother or not?"

"Well, she knows we're having open house, but I didn't go into the part about the dress. I don't think she'll go along with it, anyway."

"Don't worry," Molly said. "I'll handle it. Mothers are usually easier to convince if you don't give them too much time to think. We'll spring it on her just before it's time to go." She sprinted off ahead of me again.

Molly's plan made me uneasy, but I had to do something. The way things were looking, Weird Wayne Weston was going to become a permanent fixture around our house.

*   *   *

There was a note on the refrigerator when Molly and I got to my house that afternoon.

Jenna— They needed me for a later shift today, so you'll have to go to the open house without me. I've left sandwiches in the refrigerator. If Corey doesn't want to go, Mrs. Benevenuto says he can stay with her. I'll go right from work and meet you at school about 7:30.

XXXOOO Mom

Molly had been reading over my shoulder. "Well, so much for the plan. If your mother shows up at open house looking the way she usually does when she gets home from work, we can cross Mr. Bartholomew off the prospective husband list. You'd better start getting used to the weirdo."

The thought of having Weird Wayne as a father sent a cold front down my neck. Now that I knew Dad wasn't going to be any help, it was all up to me. "We have to do something, Molly, before it's too late. Why don't we take the dress to Mom at work? We could go over there right now. I'll see if Mrs. Benevenuto would mind having Corey a little early."

"I don't think we should bother your mother at work for this, Jenna."

"Look, Molly. This might not seem very important to you, having a normal set of parents and all, but my life is about to be ruined. The least you can do is help me carry through with the plan that was your idea in the first place."

Molly held up her hands. "Okay, okay. Don't get all bent out of shape. If you really want to do this, I'm in. Just don't blame me if your Mom kills us for interrupting her at work, that's all."

We took Corey to Mrs. Benevenuto's. She was glad to take him, so Molly and I headed for Class Memories.

"How far away is this place, anyway?" Molly asked, after we'd been walking for about fifteen minutes.

"Only a couple more blocks. I think it's that big gray building up ahead."

"I hope they're going to let us in," Molly said.

"Why wouldn't they? You visit your mother all the time at work."

"I know, but my Mom practically owns the place where she works. This is a factory. It's different."

"Well, excuse me for being a mere peasant."

"I didn't mean it that way, and you know it."

We'd reached a big building with a sign over the door that said Class Memories. In the window were dozens of pictures of kids.

Molly whistled. "Look at that. Not a zit in the whole bunch. Your mother does good work."

"If you're going to start acting smart, I'll go in alone. Give me the bag." I left Molly standing outside the double glass doors and went into the lobby.

The lady at the front desk stopped me. "May I help you with something?"

"I need to see my mother," I said. "She's a zit . . . I mean a spotter."

"Is this an emergency?"

I clutched the bag tighter. "Well, nobody's dying or anything, but I really need to talk to her."

The receptionist smiled and shoved a pencil and pad across her desk. "You just missed the afternoon break, honey, but if you'll write down your mother's name and the message, I'll see that she gets it. We can't interrupt the line unless it's a real emergency."

I took the pad and tried to think of how to put it down, but there was no way I could write a note about wanting Mom to wear a dress so she could impress Mr. Bartholomew. Besides, I needed Molly to explain it to her—in person, not in a note. I could see Molly peeking through the door. She was trying to signal me about something, but I couldn't make it out.

A delivery man pushed past me and handed a slip of paper to the receptionist. "Deliveries are in the rear," she said, without looking at it.

"This is office equipment, lady. They told me it went up here."

"Oh yes. Bring it on in and I'll show you where it goes."

I put the pad on the desk. "Thanks anyway, but I guess this can wait." I went back out to Molly. "You were right. They don't allow kids in here. Now what?"

"Did you say it was an emergency?"

"No, because it isn't. Molly, what am I going to do? Everything's going wrong lately." I started to cry.

Molly handed me a wrinkled Kleenex. "Don't fall apart now. If this means that much to you, we're going to have to get drastic." Her eyes narrowed as she watched the delivery man load some filing cabinets onto a cart. "We're going to have to sneak in."

"You can't get past that receptionist. Besides, we don't even know where Mom is," I said, blowing my nose.

"That's what I was trying to signal you about. I've been watching people go through those double doors at the back. It's one big room, like a warehouse. She has to be in there somewhere."

"What are you planning to do, crawl past old eagle-eyes on your stomach?"

"Give me that." Molly clutched the paper bag with the dress and shoes in it. "Get ready."

"For what?" I could sense one of Molly's wild schemes taking shape.

"That delivery man will be our cover. Look, she's leaving her desk to let him in."

"Oh, I see. We're going in disguised as filing cabinets. Why didn't I think of that?"

"Shh. Come on. Now!"

The receptionist was leading the delivery man down a side hall. Molly grabbed my arm and we slipped through the door, across the lobby, and through the double doors in the back. She was right. It was one huge room divided into sections with low partitions. There were people everywhere, working on various jobs. Machinery noises were coming from the far end of the room.

"Do you see her?" Molly whispered.

"Not yet. She says the pictures go by her on some sort of conveyor belt."

Molly pointed. "Those must be the conveyor belts over there. Isn't that you mother in the back row?"

I followed the direction of Molly's finger. "That's her, all right." Mom was near the middle of the room, sitting on a stool, bending over a long strip of paper that was moving past her on big rollers.

We moved around the edge of the room, staying in the shadows as long as we could. "We're going to have to crawl from here," Molly whispered. She flattened out on her stomach and started hunching along the floor like G.I. Joe. I followed. When we reached the first partition, I could see that it didn't go all the way to the floor. There was a whole row of sneakered feet on the other side. I counted them as I inched along, trying to keep myself from being scared to death. There were fifteen. Somebody must have been standing on one leg.

Then we crawled under a long table and past some big cartons until we came to Mom's purple Nikes. We were just coming up for air when Mom gasped, shoving our heads down and looking around to see if anyone was watching. "Jenna! Molly! How did you get in here?"

"It wasn't easy, believe me," Molly said, grinning.

"This may be a big joke to you two, but you could make me lose my job."

"It's really important, Mom, or we wouldn't be here, honest. It's about open house tonight."

"Didn't you see my note? I told you I'd meet you there. Darn, I missed one!" Mom was leaning way over to the right, trying to catch a zit that had slipped by.

I got up on my knees and looked at the sea of faces that was moving by on the belt. There was a big picture of each kid, with smaller ones next to it and a whole bunch of wallet-sized pictures along the bottom. All of the kids had white spots on their faces.

Molly pointed at one boy whose whole face was white dots. "Wow, look at him. He must be the zit prince of the Western world."

Mom had a tiny brush and a piece of glass with little drops of skin-colored dye on it. She was frantically poking at the white dots on the bigger pictures, making them blend into the skin. "You're distracting me. Just get out of here before somebody sees you. Rats! There goes another one." She jumped off the stool and nailed the zit prince just before he disappeared around the edge of the roller.

"We'll go right away, Mom, but I wanted to leave this package with you."

"What package?"

I looked over at Molly, hoping she'd take it from there, but she was studying some girl's hairdo and had pulled her own hair up to one side, trying to copy it. I grabbed the package from her. I could see an official-looking lady starting to come toward us from the other side of the room, so I knew there wasn't much time. "There's a dress in here, and some high heels. Put them on before you come tonight, okay?"

Mom looked up. "A dress? That's what all the fuss is about? Are you ashamed of me, Jenna? Of the way I dress?"

"No, Mom. I just want you to make a good impression, that's all." I looked to Molly for help again, but she was still doing hairdos.

"Just get out of here, both of you. And take the dress with you."

"But, Mom . . ."

"Jenna, get out of my way. I just missed an eight by ten." Mom had dropped to her knees and was trying to work on a picture that had gone over the edge of the roller.

"Here, Mom. I'll hold it back for you." I grabbed the heavy strip of pictures with both hands, and for a second it stopped moving. That's when it ripped, all the way through a big white-spotted face and right on through the wallet pictures.

"What's going on? Who let these kids in here?" A huge woman was standing over us. She looked like one of those opera singers who wear horns on their helmets and metal bras.

That brought Molly out of her trance. She grabbed my arm and we started running across the room. We never stopped until we were three blocks away from Class Memories.

"Wait," I panted, dropping down on the cement steps in front of a butcher shop. "We can't just leave her like that. We have to go back and take the blame."

Molly bit at her thumbnail. "I don't know, Jenna. I don't think we should. Nobody there knows you, right?"

"Nobody but Mom. Why?"

"Don't you see? They won't blame your mother. They don't know you're her kid, and she's not going to be dumb enough to tell them. She can just say some strange kids came in and messed her up. If we go back, they'll know she was lying, and she'll probably get fired."

"I guess you're right," I said. But a little voice in the back of my mind told me I might not be the daughter of a zit zapper much longer.

CHAPTER 8

Corey answered Mrs. Benevenuto's door when we got back. Mrs. Benevenuto was tying a bright red bandanna around Jaspar's neck. She looked up and smiled. "Ah, there you are, girls. What do you think of your handsome dog? He looks like a movie star, no?"

I was still too upset about what had happened to say anything, but Molly covered. "He looks great, Mrs. Benevenuto. He knows he's gorgeous, don't you, boy?" Molly tickled Jaspar under his chin. He showed his teeth in a doggy smile and raised one front leg so she could scratch his stomach.

"We'd better get home and eat," I said. "Thanks for watching Corey early, Mrs. Benevenuto. We'll bring him back when we leave for open house."

"Wait, don't go." Mrs. Benevenuto went over to the stove and lifted the lid on a pot that was almost as big as she was. "I've got sauce on. You girls like spaghetti?"

I hesitated by the door. A wisp of delicious steam wafted past my nose, and it looked as if she had enough sauce to feed the whole neighborhood. "Well sure, but . . ."

"Then you stay. I'll start the water boiling for pasta."

"If you're sure it's not too much trouble."

Mrs. Benevenuto filled another kettle with water and carried it over to the stove. "Trouble? Don't be silly. It seems good to cook for more than just one again. I hate to eat alone. I used to invite my neighbors over all the time after my kids grew up and moved away."

Mrs. Benevenuto shooed Molly and me out of the kitchen, but Corey stayed under the table playing with Jaspar. I could hear Mrs. Benevenuto bustling around, singing to herself as we watched her little black-and-white TV in the living room.

"Hey, is that him?" Molly asked.

I'd been staring at the screen without really seeing it. "Is that who?"

"The weirdo. Your mother's boyfriend. What's he supposed to be?"

I focused on the screen. Wayne was dressed like Peter Pan, only his whole costume was sparkly.

Every now and then he tossed a handful of glitter up in the air. "Better throw an extra log on the fire," he said in a high goofy voice. "Jack Frost is on the prowl tonight."

"Now there's a body that doesn't belong in tights," Molly said. Wayne did a little leap over the weather map, his pot belly bouncing under the skin-tight tunic. Molly practically slid off her chair, laughing.

"How can you laugh when my life is going down the tubes, Molly?"

"I'm sorry," she said, exploding into giggles again.

Luckily, Mrs. Benevenuto called us in to dinner, because I was ready to punch Molly's lights out. Pretty soon I forgot about being mad, though. Mrs. Benevenuto served the best spaghetti and sauce I had ever had. Corey dove into it like it was a mountain of egg rolls.

Mrs. Benevenuto didn't eat anything at first. She just sat there watching the rest of us. "What did you all do at school today?" She looked from face to face, beaming.

"Our gym teacher made us go out and run the track in skimpy little gym suits," Molly said.

Mrs. Benevenuto shook her head and made a clucking sound.

"We had sweat shirts on," I added. "It wasn't all that bad."

"Still," Molly said, "our legs were bare, and it's almost Thanksgiving, for pete's sake."

"I almost forgot," Corey blurted out, with three long strands of spaghetti dangling from his mouth. "I won the contest in school."

"What contest?" I asked.

Corey sucked in the spaghetti. The ends flicked spaghetti sauce freckles on his nose before disappearing. "The turkey contest. We had to write our names on a piece of paper, then put them in a big box. In assembly, they pulled one out, and it was mine." He sat back in his seat, his face flushed with excitement. "We're going to have a twenty-five-pound turkey for Thanksgiving."

Mrs. Benevenuto looked as excited as Corey. "Really? That's a nice big bird, Corey."

"He's big, all right. Well, he might not be exactly twenty-five pounds. It's hard to tell because he kept taking one foot off the scale when the principal tried to weigh him."

I almost choked on my spaghetti. "You mean he's alive?"

"Yep. They made him a big cage in the front hall. He's going to live there until we take him home for Thanksgiving."

That brought out the animal lover in Molly. "I think it's cruel to keep him caged up like that."

Corey jutted out his chin. "Is not. He loves it. A lot of the kids sneak him part of their lunches. Besides, it's not a cage. It's a big fenced-in place with lots of soft straw for Bruce to sleep on."

"Who's Bruce?" I asked.

Corey rolled his eyes. "The turkey, who else?" He turned to Mrs. Benevenuto. "You want to come to our house for Thanksgiving? We're having Bruce."

Mrs. Benevenuto laughed and patted Corey's hand. "I'm afraid I can't, Corey. My son has invited me to his house. All of his wife's relatives will be there." She made a face.

"Don't you like them?" Corey asked.

I kicked Corey under the table. "That's none of your business," I said.

Mrs. Benevenuto shook her head. "No, it's all right. It's just that my daughter-in-law isn't Italian."

Corey reached down to rub the spot I had connected with on his ankle. "We're nice, and I don't think we're Italian. Are we Italian, Jenna?"

"Corey! Knock it off."

"I didn't mean that the way it sounded," Mrs. Benevenuto said. "It's just the traditions I miss.

Thanksgiving with antipasto, minestrone, lasagna, manicotti, cannolis."

"No turkey?" Molly asked.

Mrs. Benevenuto shrugged. "Oh sure, turkey too, but the other things make it special for me. Always I used to cook a big Thanksgiving meal for my family. It was a way to show them how much I loved them." She pulled her tiny body up tall in her seat. "Now we have the dinners at my son's house because they have the space and the big dining room. They don't even let me help in the kitchen."

"Maybe you could take something along with you when you go on Thanksgiving," I suggested. "One of those special things you used to make."

"That's a good idea, Jenna." Her face started to brighten. "Just a little something maybe. Not much, not enough to insult my daughter-in-law that she's not a good cook. Just a little something . . ."

She sort of faded off, nodding and smiling to herself. I was so full I was feeling sleepy until the grandfather clock chimed—seven times.

Molly jumped up from the table. "We're late. I told Mom and Dad I'd meet them at open house at seven."

"Go ahead, girls," Mrs. Benevenuto said. "I'll

have some dessert for you when you get back."

Molly and I thanked her and headed out for school. We practically ran all the way. Where was old Ms. Raskin with her stopwatch when you wanted her? When we got there, the place was packed.

"Keep a lookout for your mom," Molly said. "If she's getting anywhere near Mr. Bartholomew, we should head her off."

"I'm not sure I want to get anywhere near Mom myself," I said. "She's going to be really steamed about what we did."

Molly bit her lip. "But we were just trying to help. She'll understand."

"Molly, there you are." Molly's mother appeared in the crowd, looking like a model out of a magazine, followed by her distinguished-looking husband. "Jenna, dear. How are . . . things?" She held out her hands with the beautiful manicured nails, not like Mom's—all stained with paint or dye.

"Just fine, Mrs. Welter."

"I've been looking for your mother. Is she here?"

"Um . . . not yet. She had to work late."

"Where is she working, dear? We haven't had a chance to talk in weeks. Last time we did she said she was . . . between jobs."

How do you tell a lawyer and a vice president of something-or-other that your mother is a zit zapper? Molly came to the rescue. "She has a real arty job, Mom. You know how talented Mrs. Bryant is. Anyway, come on. I want you both to meet my English teacher."

I wandered around the crowded halls for another ten minutes, looking for Mom. Finally, I spotted her coming through the front door, but before I could get to her, Molly showed up again.

"I left Mom and Dad with Mrs. Aiken. She can keep them talking for an hour. I thought you'd need my help with . . . oh-oh! There she is."

Mom was wearing jeans and her bright green ski jacket. Her long hair was flying in all directions, and her cheeks were bright red from the cold. Molly had been right. Mom was a mess. She spotted us and started working her way through the crowd.

"That's amazing," Molly whispered.

"What's amazing?"

Molly watched Mom as she came toward us. "Well, she's not dressed up or anything, but she doesn't look bad. She sort of has that windblown effect they use with fashion models in the magazines."

"Windblown! She looks like the lone survivor of a tornado."

Molly was squinting at Mom and nodding. "She's really quite pretty. If Mr. Bartholomew is the athletic type, this might be just the look he'd go for. She looks like a skier, don't you think?"

I grabbed Molly's shoulder and turned her around to face me. "Do you mean after all the trouble we went through to take that stupid dress to Mom, you think she looks great in her regular stuff?"

Mom got to us before Molly had a chance to answer. She shoved the paper bag at Molly. "I think you forgot this."

"Mom, I'm really sorry. . ."

"Never mind," Mom snapped, her lips set in a tight line. "I want to talk to your math teacher. That's the course you're having the most trouble with, isn't it?"

"Yes, well, sort of." I couldn't let her meet Mr. Bartholomew when she was in a mood like this. "Actually, math has been pretty good lately."

She pulled a wad of folded papers out of her pocket. "You call this pretty good?" It was the bunch of math quizzes I had taken home last week. The one on top had a big 57 written across the top in red. And that was one of the better ones.

The math room was only two doors down the hall, but I started leading Mom in the wrong direction, hoping that by the time we circled around the whole school, she'd have cooled down. It didn't work. When we came around the last corner, she recognized the hall.

"This is where we started from. Did you actually think you could keep me away from this teacher by taking me on a wild goose chase all over the school?" She stormed down the hall ahead of me, reading the nameplates on the classroom doors. "This one says 'Mr. Bartholomew—Math,'" she yelled back to me. "Is this it?"

By the time I caught up to her, Mr. Bartholomew and a set of parents were staring open-mouthed at the wild-haired woman in the doorway. Mr. Bartholomew seemed relieved when he saw me. He came to the door. "You must be Jenna's mother," he said.

Mom brushed a hunk of hair out of her eyes and pulled the wad of math quizzes from her pocket. "Yes, I wanted to talk to you about these."

The thick folded pile flipped open, and half of the papers fell on the floor. Mom and Mr. Bartholomew both bent down to pick them up at the same time. Then a terrible thing happened. They clunked heads so hard that Mr. Bartholomew lost his balance and sprawled backward on the floor. I couldn't believe it!

Mom reached out to help him up. "I'm sorry. Are you all right?"

Mr. Bartholomew waved her away and struggled to his feet, red-faced. "I'm fine."

"I feel terrible," Mom said, clawing the hunk of hair out of her face again. "Things like this have been happening to me all day."

Mr. Bartholomew gave her one of his toothpaste commercial smiles. "I know what you mean. I've had a pretty bad day myself. If you'll just give me a minute, I'll finish up with the Abernathys, and then we can talk about Jenna."

Maybe this could work out after all. Mom hadn't made the best first impression in the world, but at least he had noticed her. Now, if they would just talk about something besides math—maybe the bad days they both had had or their favorite sports or something.

I watched Mom as she wandered around the room looking at the things on the bulletin boards. Molly was right. Mom looked kind of pretty, even though she wasn't perfect like Mrs. Welter. Maybe Mr. Bartholomew didn't even like perfect. Maybe because he had to do everything perfectly in math, he'd rather have a wife who goofed up sometimes. Mom would be great at that. She practically specialized in goofing up.

The Abernathys finally got up and headed for the door, with Mrs. Abernathy giving Mom a strange look. Mr. Bartholomew motioned for Mom to sit down at his desk. I watched them from across the room. They looked good together. They smiled and laughed for a few minutes; then the talk got more serious. They were looking intently into each other's eyes as they spoke. It looked like love at first sight.

I tried to imagine what it would be like if they got married. At least he was handsome, like Dad. Mr. Bartholomew even looked a little bit like Dad, except for the hair color. I couldn't ever call him Dad, though. Maybe Father.

I pretended that Mr. Bartholomew's desk was our dining room table. I went over and slipped quietly into the seat next to Mom. The paper in front of me was my plate, and I arranged a pen and a couple of pencils like silverware. I watched Mr. Bartholomew as he talked to Mom. His eyes were so blue, and he had a dimple on his right cheek when he smiled. I was sure he could have been a TV star if he hadn't decided to be a teacher instead.

A pile of books in the middle of the desk became a Thanksgiving turkey, and Mr. Bartholomew—Father—was going to carve it. I could almost smell the turkey as I fingered a small dish of paper clips —the cranberry sauce. Suddenly I realized Mr. . . . Father was talking to me.

"What?" I asked.

"Which would you prefer?"

"Oh, white meat, please."

"Jenna!" Mom's hand came down on my shoulder. "Are you listening to anything that's being said here?" The cozy family scene evaporated. "Mr. Bartholomew just asked you if you'd rather come before school or after for extra help."

"Extra help?"

Mr. Bartholomew moved the cranberry sauce out of my reach. "I think it's the best solution right now, Jenna. It's mainly fractions that still seem to be giving you trouble. If you can come in here every day, either before homeroom or after last period, I think we can clear up your confusion in no time."

"Oh." That wasn't going to do any good. Mom was the one who needed to get together with Mr. Bartholomew, not me. Then I had a brilliant idea. "But I have to watch my little brother after school, Mr. Bartholomew. Could you come to our house instead of me coming here?"

"Jenna," Mom said, "teachers don't make house calls."

Mr. Bartholomew laughed. "I'm afraid your mother's right. I'll be working with several students at a time. You're not the only one who finds fractions a mystery, Jenna. Will it be before homeroom, then?"

What choice did I have? "Sure."

Mr. Bartholomew stood up and reached out to shake Mom's hand. "It's been a pleasure meeting you, Mrs. Bryant. If you ever have any questions, please don't hesitate to call."

So much for the big romance. He could have been talking to somebody's grandmother, for pete's sake. And now, not only was I *not* getting a new father, I'd be having an extra dose of math every day.

I might not be too good at fractions, but I knew if you took one quarter of a family away, you'd have three quarters of a family left, and that's what we were stuck with. A lousy three quarters of a family. And adding Weird Wayne to it wasn't going to make it whole again.

When we left Mr. Bartholomew's room, Molly was waiting in the hall. She fell in step with me as Mom strode on ahead toward the door. "Well, how did it go? Did they hit it off?"

"They hit it off, all right," I mumbled. "She knocked him right off his feet."

Mom didn't say anything on the way to the car. She drove out of the parking lot, then slammed on the brakes and pulled over to the curb. She turned to look at me, her eyes shiny in the light from the streetlamp. "Are you ashamed of me, Jenna? Because if you are, I want to have this out right now."

"Why would I be ashamed?"

Mom's hands gripped the steering wheel. "I'm doing my best, you know. I'm trying very hard to keep this family afloat, and you're not making it any easier for me."

"If you mean about coming over to where you work, Mom, I'm really sorry. It won't happen again."

"I can guarantee that, Jenna. Do you know why?" Her voice cracked at the end, and she didn't give me a chance to answer. "It won't happen again because I'm not working at Class Memories anymore."

"You got fired?" I gasped.

"No, *I* didn't get fired. I finally found a job that I could manage—one that I was even good at—until my daughter and her little friend came in and caused such a scene *they* got me fired." She smacked the steering wheel hard, then slumped forward and pressed her forehead against it.

"That's awful. It's not fair that they fired you because of what we did."

Mom turned back to me, and I could see her cheeks were wet with tears. "You're right, it's not fair. It's also not fair that I'm trying to raise two kids on minimum-wage jobs, and my ex-husband is sending me support checks whenever he happens to think of it, which is practically never. Life isn't fair, Jenna. Got that? You might as well learn it now and get used to it."

"But that's not Dad's fault, Mom. It's because Gladys spends all his money."

"Your father is an adult, Jenna. He's responsible for his own decisions, so don't go dumping all the blame on that blonde bombshell. I'm sure she has enough problems just being married to him. I know I did."

She started the car and gunned the engine down the street. I hated it when she talked about Dad like that. She just didn't understand him the way I did. As if things weren't bad enough, there was a familiar-looking beat-up car waiting as we pulled into our driveway.

"Wayne's here," Mom said. She wiped her eyes and looked in the rear-view mirror while she ran her fingers through her hair. "I forgot he was coming over tonight."

"Me too," I said. "You go ahead, Mom. I'll get Corey." I figured maybe Wayne would be gone by the time I got back.

Mrs. Benevenuto had this delicious thing called a cannoli that she'd saved for me. She and Corey and Jaspar had already eaten theirs, and they all watched me while I ate mine. Jaspar kept waiting for me to drop a crumb, but I didn't. When we left

Mrs. Benevenuto's apartment, I could see that Wayne's car was still in the driveway. I should have killed more time.

Jaspar bounded ahead on the leash, and Corey was still babbling about the cannolis. "They look a lot like egg rolls, don't they, Jen? I think that's why I like them so much. They're like egg rolls, only with dessert inside."

Corey and Jaspar spotted Wayne the minute we got inside the house. "Wayne! You look neat-o! How's Ranger Ralph? Did you tell him hello for me again?" They both jumped up on the couch next to Wayne.

"Sure did," Wayne said. He was in his regular clothes, but he had silver makeup with pointy ears, and his hair was sprayed white with glitter all over it. "And I gave a big hello to Dr. Molar from Jaspar. He sent a message to you, Jaspar—'Woof, woof. . . grrr . . . yippity-yip.'"

Jaspar jumped down from the couch with a whimper and went over in the corner of the living room.

Wayne turned to Mom and wiggled his eyebrows. A few sparkles drifted down on his shoulders like dandruff. "Look at Jaspar. Dr. Molar's message must have been some sort of canine insult." Mom and Corey laughed as usual. Wayne folded his hands over his fat stomach and looked up at me. "How are things going for you, Jenna?"

"I have lots of homework," I said and headed for the stairs. My life was really going downhill. Before, I thought there was nothing worse than being the daughter of a zit zapper. Now I was the daughter of an unemployed zit zapper who was dating a jerk. That was definitely worse.

CHAPTER 9

It wasn't until the morning before Thanksgiving that Corey mentioned the turkey again. Mom was mad that he told her at the last minute, but Corey said he forgot because he'd been so busy. He'd been busy, all right. First Wayne took him to watch the Ranger Ralph Show. Then, when he told some of his classmates about it, they wanted to go too, so Wayne took Corey the next week with three of his friends. Ever since then Corey had been getting pretty popular at school, and most of the phone calls we got were for him. I was glad he'd stopped being a hermit, but now he was going overboard.

Anyway, Mom called the school, and they said the janitor would be there until five, so we could pick up the turkey.

"There he is. There's Bruce." Corey practically dragged Mom across the front hall of his school. A big corner section of the hall was fenced off with chicken wire and filled with straw. In the center of the pen a huge white turkey pecked at a chocolate Twinkie. Corey squatted close to the chicken wire.

The janitor was sweeping nearby and came over to us. "You must be Mrs. Bryant. I'm Ed. Came to pick up the bird that Corey won, right?"

Mom couldn't stop staring at Bruce, and Bruce stared back at her between beakfuls of Twinkie. "Yes, Ed, but I thought when we came to get him he'd be already . . . um . . . you know."

"Dead?"

Mom winced and nodded.

"Naw. Got the name of a feller can dress him out for you, though. Friend of my brother's just east of the city, out in the town of Ontario." He fished a crumpled piece of paper out of his pocket. "Here it is—Jack Hatch on Knickerbocker Road." He handed it to Mom.

"But how do we get him there?" Mom asked.

"It's all right there. I drew a map and every-thing. Can't miss it. I'll call ahead and tell 'im you'll be coming if you want. He gets pretty busy this time of year."

"I didn't mean how do we get there," Mom said, still staring at the turkey. "I meant how do we get Bruce there?"

Corey ran over to us. "He can sit in back with me, Mommy. I'll make sure he keeps his seat belt fastened the whole time, I promise."

Ed grunted. "I think we'd better wrap this bird up for you. Turkeys ain't much for travelin' in cars." With one deft motion, he slipped a feed sack over Bruce's legs and pulled it up to his neck. Then he wound a rope loosely around Bruce's neck to hold the sack in place and carried him out to the car for us. He put Bruce in my lap in the front seat. "Hang onto 'im, hear? The sack should keep 'im from jumping around, but turkeys ain't much for travelin' in cars."

Bruce weighed a ton, and I could feel him shuffling his feet around, trying to get comfortable on my lap. He didn't smell real great, either.

"It's not fair," Corey howled from the back as we took off. "Bruce is my turkey. I won him and everything, not Jenna."

Mom looked at Corey in the rear-view mirror. "He's much too heavy for you, Corey. I can't take any chances on him getting loose while I drive."

Bruce seemed to be lulled by the sound of the car's engine and stayed perfectly still until we got out of the city. Then we came to a stop sign and Mom had to check Ed's map. Bruce started watching the cars going back and forth in front of us through the intersection. He looked like the referee at a Ping-Pong match.

Mom leaned forward to see around him. "For

heaven's sake, Jenna. What's wrong with that
bird?"

"He's just watching the traffic for you, Mom, like
Dad used to do. He'll tell you when to go."

Mom spotted a hole in the traffic and gunned the
engine. "Sorry, Bruce, old boy, but I'm not taking
orders from a turkey. I did that for too many years."

"Hey, Bruce, look back here." Corey was peeking over the top of my seat. Bruce swiveled his
head around so his beak was about three inches
from my nose. He was cross-eyed.

"Doesn't he have beautiful waffles?" Corey
asked.

"Waffles?" I asked.

"That pretty red and blue thing that hangs down
off his beak."

"That's wattles, you turkey," I yelled. That was a
mistake because it got Bruce excited. He swiveled
again and made a high-pitched gobbling sound in
his throat. Then Corey laughed and Bruce gobbled, and Mom yelled and Bruce gobbled again,
and we all started laughing and Bruce gobbled
nonstop.

We came to another intersection. Mom scrubbed
at the windshield with her mitten. "Open your
window, Jenna. We've steamed up the glass so
much I can't see the name of the road."

I rolled down my window, but Bruce stuck his

head out first. "It's Knick something," I said, straining to see around the rubber-necked bird.

"Great. Keep an eye out for a white house and red barn. There should be two big pine trees out front. What on earth is that turkey doing?"

"I think he's signaling for a right-hand turn," I said. "Hey, there it is. The next house."

As we pulled into the driveway, a man in blood-stained coveralls came out from behind the barn. Bruce pulled in his head and got suddenly quiet.

The man ducked down to look in my window. "I'm Jack Hatch. You the ones Ed called about?"

"Yes, Mr. Hatch," Mom said, leaning across to my side of the seat. "I'm glad we found the right place. It was quite a trip."

"Expect so. Turkey's ain't much for travelin' in cars." He opened the door and took Bruce. "I'll have him dressed out for you in no time. Shouldn't be more'n fifteen, twenty minutes. You can come watch if you want."

"Could we, Mom?" Corey shouted. "Please?"

Mom shuddered. "No, Corey. We'll wait right here."

"Suit yourself," Mr. Hatch said. We watched him disappear behind the barn with Bruce peering innocently over his shoulder. I tried not to think about what was about to happen. I couldn't believe

Corey had wanted to watch. Bruce had been pretty nice for a turkey.

Corey hung over my seat. "Tomorrow is Thanksgiving, Mommy. Are we having a Thanksgiving dinner like the Pilgrims and the Indians?"

Mom leaned her head back and rubbed her forehead. "Sure, Corey. We're having a regular Thanksgiving dinner with turkey and cranberry sauce, just like we always have."

"Neato!" Corey squealed, using the back seat for a trampoline. Then he draped himself over the front seat again. "When do we go get the turkey?"

Mom's eyes grew wide. "Corey, I thought you understood. Bruce *is* our Thanksgiving turkey."

"I know. But I meant, when do we go get the meat turkey? The one we're going to eat."

Mom pulled Corey over the seat and squeezed him onto her lap behind the steering wheel. "Honey, why do you think we brought Bruce here?"

"So he could get fixed up for Thanksgiving dinner."

Mom rested her cheek in Corey's hair, "Yes, but fixed up . . . how?"

Corey thought for a minute. "Well, he'll probably have a bath and get his toenails cleaned. He has yucky toenails. Then Ed said Mr. Hatch is going to

dress him up." He giggled. "I wonder what old
Bruce is going to look like in clothes, Mommy. Do
you think he's going to have a hat? Does Mr. Hatch
have all kinds of turkey clothes?"

Mom groaned softly. "Listen, Corey. I thought
you understood that Mr. Hatch is getting Bruce
ready so that on Thanksgiving we can..." Mom
glanced over at me for help, but I turned away and
looked out the window. She'd have to get herself
out of this one.

"So we can what, Mommy?" Corey asked.

"So we can, um... eat... him."

Corey's scream bounced off the walls of the car
like an electric saw hitting metal. He pushed past
Mom, opened the car door, and started running for
the barn. Mom and I took off after him, and we all
rounded the corner of the barn at the same time.
What we saw made my stomach turn over.

Mr. Hatch had a big pot of boiling water hanging
over a wood fire. And there, tied upside down to
the branch of a big tree, was a headless half-naked
white turkey. It twisted slowly on the rope with hot
water dripping from what was left of its feathers.

"I want Bruce!" Corey shrieked, shoving Mr.
Hatch away from the dangling bird.

There was fresh blood on Mr. Hatch's coveralls,
and damp white feathers clung to his hands. "Tar-
nation! I told you'd it'd be at least fifteen minutes.

You city folk have no patience at all. I ain't no danged machine, you know. This takes time."

Corey was in a heap on the ground, sobbing over a clump of steaming white feathers. Mom gathered him up in her arms.

Mr. Hatch scratched his head, leaving some white fluff in his wool cap. "What's wrong with the little feller?"

"He didn't know his turkey was going to be killed," Mom shouted over Corey's screams. "It's my fault. I didn't explain."

"Well, for land sakes, I'd better not kill him, then." He pointed to the barn. "There he is. Take him on home. This here bird belongs to some other folks, and they'll be here any minute to pick it up."

There, huddled against the barn, was Bruce, still in his feed sack. "Bruce! You're alive," Corey squealed. He ran over and threw his arms around the startled bird.

"Did you let Bruce watch while you... murdered this other poor turkey?" Mom asked, her eyes narrowing.

Mr. Hatch snorted. "What did you want me to do, lady? Blindfold him?"

"That's the most inhumane thing I ever heard of. He's probably damaged for life." She marched over and scooped Bruce up into her arms like a baby. "Come on, kids. We're getting out of here."

Mr. Hatch called after us. "You city folks get nuttier all the time. Stick to them Butterballs from now on."

Corey was still crying when we got to the car. The only way Mom could get him to shut up was to put Bruce into the seat next to him.

"He can't be just loose back here, Corey," Mom said, pulling the seat belt around Bruce. She tried to tighten it, but it slipped right off. "This isn't working. You can't put a seat belt on something that doesn't have a lap. Wait a minute. I have an idea." She got out and started shuffling through the junk in the trunk of the car. "There. I thought I still had this back there." She plunked Corey's old car seat into the car and fastened it down with the seat belt. Then she squeezed Bruce into the seat, tucking the sack in around him.

"This is never going to work, Mom," I said. "Do you want me to get in the back and hold him?"

"No. Just me and Bruce are going to be back here," Corey said. "You got to hold him all the way out."

Mom pulled the shoulder straps tight over Bruce's chest and fastened them in front. Then she lowered the padded bar over him. "Perfect!" she announced, closing the door and sliding in front with me.

"I don't believe this," I said. "What are we going to do now?"

Mom started the car and pulled out of the driveway. "That's what I wanted to talk to Corey about. Corey, what would you think of finding a nice home for Bruce?"

Corey had stopped crying, but his breath was still coming in little shudders. "We have a nice home. He can live in our nice home."

Mom smiled into the rear-view mirror. I recognized the look. It was her old "I'm-going-to-be-nice-and-calm-and-talk-him-into-this" smile. She'd used it on me a million times, and she usually won. "Turkeys aren't happy living in houses, Corey."

"They aren't?" Score one for Mom.

"No, a turkey needs to live on a farm in order to be really happy."

"Mr. Hatch has a farm, and he does terrible things to turkeys." Score one for Corey.

"But I'm thinking of a special kind of farm. A place where the people are very kind to animals—all kinds of animals."

"Really? What kind of farm is that?" Corey one. Mom two.

"It's called Lollipop Farm, and they take in all kinds of stray animals. There's even a petting zoo where we could go visit Bruce."

"Bruce would love that. Do they really grow lollipops? Bruce loves Tootsie Pops."

Bingo!

Mom checked her watch. "It's getting a little late, but I think we can just about get there before it closes."

She made a few wrong turns, but pretty soon we were headed down the right road. Bruce didn't seem to mind the baby car seat. He kept looking out the windows at the lights that were starting to go on in the houses we passed. Everything was going pretty well, until we heard the police siren.

Mom groaned. She pulled over, and the police car stopped behind us.

Corey got up on his knees, so he could see out the back window. "Wow, Mommy. Look at the policeman with a real cowboy hat. He looks just like Ranger Ralph. Do you think that's who it is, Mommy?"

"No, Corey. He's a county sheriff. Just be quiet."

She rolled down her window.

"You know how fast you were going, lady?" One side of the policeman's face flashed red from the lights on his car. He glanced at the back seat, then did a double take and leaned down for a closer look.

"I'm sorry," Mom said. "I guess I may have been going a little fast. I have a lot on my mind and . . .

Well, I know that isn't an excuse for speeding...
I'm usually so careful... but we've had this really,
well, unusual day and now we're trying to get
to..."

"Lady, do you mind telling me what you have in
your back seat?"

"That? Oh. Well, that's what I meant about this
unusual experience. You see it all started when
we..."

Corey leaned over the front seat. "That's Bruce.
He's my little brother. I thought you were Ranger
Ralph, but you don't look like him up close. Did he
let you have his hat?"

The sheriff took a closer look at Bruce. Bruce
jerked his head around to get a better look at the
sheriff, his wattles quivering in the red light.

"Hush, Corey," Mom said. "Bruce is our turkey,
officer."

The sheriff grinned. "That's a relief. I was thinking you had about the ugliest baby I'd ever seen.
So... you folks just out taking the turkey for a
ride?"

Mom sighed and nodded. "Something like that."

He shook his head. I think he thought Mom had
escaped from a nut house. "Well, I'll let you go this
time, but keep track of your speed from now on."

"Thank you, officer. I'll be careful."

He tipped his hat and bent down for one last

look at Bruce. "Darndest thing I ever saw. Turkeys usually ain't much for travelin' in cars."

From then on Mom drove so slowly, every car on the road passed us. She never did anything half-way. She drove so slowly in fact that Lollipop Farm was closed by the time we got there. And when we finally got back home, with Bruce still in the car seat, the grocery store was closed, too.

"Now what are we going to do?" I said, slamming the car door. "We can't have Thanksgiving dinner without a turkey."

"We have a turkey," Corey piped up from the back seat.

"To eat, dummy!" I shouted.

Mom brushed the hair back out of her eyes. "Jenna, this isn't the end of the world. I have a chicken in the freezer. I'll make stuffing and we'll have cranberry sauce. You won't even know the difference. A big turkey would have been too much for just the three of us, anyway."

She was right. Why bother to have a whole Thanksgiving dinner when you were only three quarters of a family? Why bother to do anything special anymore? Mom just couldn't manage by herself, and now that she was out of a job again, things would be getting even worse. Dad might have done some stupid things, but he never got chased by a sheriff while he was speeding with a turkey in a car seat.

There was a loud gobble from the back seat.

"Shut up, Bruce," I yelled.

That just made him gobble again.

CHAPTER 10

After all of the excitement the night before, I slept late Thanksgiving morning. It was the phone that finally woke me up. Dad! He said he'd call, and he kept his promise. I ran into Mom's room to answer it, but Mom had already picked it up in the kitchen. And it wasn't Dad. It was just Mrs. Benevenuto, so I hung up without saying anything. I hoped Mom wouldn't stay on the line with her too long in case Dad was trying to call.

Mom was off the phone by the time I got down to the kitchen. She was putting something strange into the roasting pan.

"What the heck is that? It looks like a porcupine."

"Don't be critical," Mom said. "It's our Thanksgiving chicken."

"What are those things sticking out all over it?"

"Toothpicks." The thing started to come apart in

Mom's hands. It landed in a heap in the roasting pan, with stuffing spilling out of the sides. "Darn. I had this all put together once. Now I'll have to start over."

"You said you had a chicken. That's chicken parts."

"It's the same thing," Mom said. "The only trouble is, when you put chicken parts back together, you don't end up with a whole chicken. At least I didn't." She started to reassemble the meat sculpture, poking the stuffing inside and skewering it with more toothpicks.

"That looks really gross, Mom. Besides, we're going to choke to death on all those toothpicks."

"Jenna, I'm doing my best to make this a real Thanksgiving. Try to be more flexible, will you? Why are you such a grouch this morning?"

I poured myself a bowl of cereal. "Look, I'm the one with the room right next to the bathroom. Every time Bruce gobbled in that shower stall, it sounded as if a herd of turkeys was coming through my wall. I don't think I slept more than an hour all night."

"Well, you slept long enough this morning to make up for it. It's almost eleven, you know. We'll take Bruce to Lollipop Farm first thing tomorrow morning, but for now I'm afraid we're stuck with him. Darn!" The chicken thing had collapsed again.

Mom went to the refrigerator and pulled out a package of hamburger.

"What are you going to do with that?"

"Repair the chicken, what else?"

She started filling in the gaps with hunks of hamburger, smoothing it out to hide the seams. Pretty soon it started to look sort of like a whole chicken, except it was yellow in the chicken parts and red in the hamburger parts.

"I didn't get an A in sculpture class for nothing." She gave her meat thing a final pat and held up the pan. "There, what do you think?"

"It looks like a cross between Chicken McNuggets and a Big Mac," I said.

Mom slipped it into the oven. "You have no imagination, Jenna. Hurry up and get dressed. Mrs. Benevenuto called a few minutes ago and asked if you could come over and help her with something."

I finished breakfast and went upstairs to get dressed. The bathroom door was closed. "Open up, Corey. I want to brush my teeth."

"You can come in, Jenna. Me and Bruce are just playing."

I didn't feel like facing Bruce right after breakfast, so I skipped the teeth.

"I'm going next door, Mom. Be sure and send Corey over for me if Dad calls."

"I don't think there's much chance of that, Jenna. Holidays are just like any other day to your father."

"No really, he's calling today. He promised."

Mom sighed and looked at me. "Just don't get your hopes up. You'll only be disappointed."

"Why do you always put him down?" I yelled, and slammed the door before she could answer.

Mrs. Benevenuto greeted me with a big smile. "Ah, Jenna. Happy Thanksgiving." She was wearing a black silky dress with a string of pearls, and she even had some pink lipstick on. Her hair was twisted up the back with a pouf of silver curls on the top.

"Hi, Mrs. Benevenuto. You look really nice. Mom said you need some help."

She fingered her hair nervously. "Thank you, Jenna. The bulb burned out in the ceiling light in my kitchen. If I hold the chair for you, do you suppose you could put a new one in for me?"

"Sure, no problem." As I was screwing in the bulb, I heard the distinct sound of footsteps over my head. "Do you have company?"

Mrs. Benevenuto held my hand as I jumped down. "It's Vincent, that nice Italian boy who used to live here. He and his friends in the band came to pick up the things he stored in my attic."

The footsteps got louder as they came down the stairs. I was curious because I'd never seen Vin-

cent's band before. There were three of them, and
they had bright-colored hair that stood straight out
from their heads. I mean *real* colors, like green,
purple, and blue. Vincent had dyed his hair shocking pink and his beard school-bus yellow.

"Do you remember little Jenna Bryant from next
door, Vincent?"

The pink head nodded over the carton he was
carrying. "Sure. How's it goin', kid?"

"Great," I said. Boy, I sure wished Molly was
here to see this.

Mrs. Benevenuto beamed. "Vincent said his
band is playing a jig in New York City. Imagine
that."

"A gig," Blue Hair said.

"Beg pardon?"

"It's a gig, Mrs. Benevenuto," Vincent said,
grinning. "That's what a band calls a job. Anyway,
watch for us on MTV, kid. We're hitting the big
time."

"That's great," I said.

"We're going to take this stuff over to my apartment and come back for the last load, Mrs. B., if
that's all right with you."

"That's fine, Vincent. I won't be leaving for a
while."

They all trooped out. Vincent gave me a high

five on the way out and almost dropped his carton.

"I thought you'd be at your son's already, Mrs. Benevenuto," I said.

"No, they have dinner late in the day. Tony will be here to pick me up about two."

"You look like you're more excited about it than you were a while back."

Mrs. Benevenuto patted her refrigerator door. "I took your advice and made a little little something to take along. Now it seems like a real Thanksgiving."

Just then the phone rang. "Hello? Yes, Joseph? . . . He did? . . . No . . ." She made that clucking noise into the phone. "Are you sure it wasn't just an accident? . . . Oh, that's terrible. I'm glad you warned me."

"Is something wrong, Mrs. Benevenuto?" I asked, after she had hung up.

"That was Joseph Felty, my old neighbor from Sodus. His goat went into the barn."

"That's it? The goat's in the barn?"

"You don't understand. This is no ordinary goat. The only time he ever goes into the barn is when he knows a big storm is coming up."

I laughed. "You're kidding. How does a goat know there's going to be a storm?"

She shook her finger at me. "Don't make fun of

nature, Jenna. Animals know things we couldn't begin to understand. Remember the blizzard of '77?"

"Not really."

"Well, it was a dandy, believe me. The only reason our town didn't get caught by surprise is that Joseph Felty's goat gave us enough warning to get supplies in."

"You mean other people in the town believe in this goat, too?"

"Sure. He's predicted lots of storms, and even a hurricane once. Now, when Joseph's goat goes into the barn, they close the Sodus schools. They'd close them today if it wasn't already a holiday." She went to the phone. "I'm going to pack a nightgown and call Tony to come get me early, before the storm starts."

"Well, good-bye, Mrs. Benevenuto. Have a nice Thanksgiving. I'll see you after the big blizzard."

"I can see you don't believe me, Jenna, but you will. Just wait."

When I got back home, Wayne was in the living room, having the last-minute fitting on his turkey costume. I couldn't even get away from him on a holiday, for pete's sake.

"Look at Wayne, Jenna. Doesn't he look a lot like Bruce?" Corey asked.

"They could be brothers," I said.

Mom was pinning felt wattles to Wayne's beak. "I must admit, it helped to have a live model for the last-minute touches."

Wayne changed out of his costume, and Mom put the final stitches in the wattles. "There," she said, folding the costume into a big bag for him. "You'd better get going. Where did you say you were having Thanksgiving dinner?"

"At my brother's house out in Gates," Wayne said. "I should just about have time to get out there and back between the noon update and the six o'clock news."

I remembered Joseph Felty's goat and decided to give Wayne a little weather test. "Hey, Wayne, is there a big snowstorm coming this way?"

"There was nothing on the weather map to indicate snow, Jenna. As a matter of fact, I'm predicting some sun for this afternoon."

As I watched him head for his car, the first few snowflakes came circling lazily down. Score one for the goat.

I went up to Mom's room and called Molly. She was excited because they were going to a big dinner with all their relatives, and her cute cousin, Adam, would be there. She went on about him for so long, I could barely get a word into the conversation.

"Molly!" I finally interrupted. "Could we talk about *my* problem for a change?"

"What problem?"

"Wayne, who else? He was even over here today. How am I going to get rid of him?"

"Oh, I don't know, Jenna. Shove him off a bridge or something. Listen, not only is Adam on the soccer and wrestling teams, but he's an expert skier, too. And he has the most beautiful eyes."

"Some best friend you are," I said. "You don't even care that my life is falling apart."

"Don't exaggerate. You'll just have to get used to Wayne. But getting back to Adam..."

"Forget it, Molly. I think somebody should tell you, it's against the law to marry your cousin." I hung up the phone and went downstairs. Almost an hour had gone by since Wayne left.

"Wow, Mom. Look at all the snow."

"I know. There must be six inches already," Mom said. "I don't think I ever saw it come down this fast. The sky's getting so dark." Jaspar whined by the back door. "Will you take the dog out, Jenna? He's been teasing, and I'm up to my elbows in cranberry sauce."

I bundled up in heavy clothes and boots and took him out. Jaspar bounded into the back yard like a puppy, his ears flying straight up with each leap. He loved snow. I knew it would take him longer to find his spot, though, because he couldn't do it by scent.

I went over to the fence and looked down Russell Street. For the first time since we'd moved here, it was beautiful. There were lots of evergreen trees on both sides of the street, and it looked as if someone had gone over each branch with a big tube of white frosting. Then I noticed that the lights were on in Mrs. Benevenuto's apartment. I closed the gate behind me and went to check on her.

"Come in, Jenna." She looked as if she'd been crying. The curls on top of her head had come partly unpinned and flopped to one side.

"I thought you'd be gone by now, Mrs. Benevenuto. Didn't you call your son?"

"I called and told him about Joseph Felty's goat, but he just laughed at me. 'Let go of those silly superstitions, Mama,' he said. 'Weathermen are a lot smarter than goats.' My son makes fun of the old ways."

I could think of a weatherman that didn't have the brains of a turkey, let alone a goat, but I didn't say anything. "Well, Tony will still come to get you, right? You won't leave as early, but you'll get there."

She shook her head, knocking a few more curls out of place. "He just called back to say the roads are so bad he doesn't think he should start out. He says they'll save the turkey and heat it up again tomorrow, but I should stay here for today. You can't do that to a turkey. It'll be dry as a bone. My daughter-in-law is no cook." Her lower lip started to tremble. "And I don't think she's so wild about her mother-in-law, either."

"You shouldn't stay here all by yourself, Mrs. Benevenuto. Come on over and have Thanksgiving with us."

"That's nice of you, Jenna, but I don't want to impose."

"No, really. It would be nice to have you come."

I helped her get bundled up and took her over to our part of the house. The snow was even deeper than it had been when I first came out, and I had to hang onto her so she wouldn't fall.

Mom was still stirring the cranberry sauce over the stove when we came in. "Mrs. Benevenuto couldn't go to her son's because of the storm, Mom. I invited her to have dinner with us."

Mom smiled. "Fine. The more, the merrier. Why don't you go into the living room and relax, Mrs. Benevenuto. I think one of the parades is still going."

I tried to cheer Mrs. Benevenuto up by talking about all the parade floats, but she ignored the TV and sat by the window, watching the snow.

A little while later the doorbell rang, and Corey went to answer it. "Wayne, you're back!"

Mom came in from the kitchen. "What happened? I thought you were going to your brother's."

"I was, but this storm started up out of nowhere. I didn't dare take a chance on not getting back in time. Besides, I had a little problem with my turkey head on the noon show. The weight of the beak and wattles pulled it forward over my eyes, and a blind turkey makes a lousy weatherman. Could you take a look at it for me?"

Mom laughed. "Sure. You might as well stay for dinner, too. It's probably not going to be the greatest Thanksgiving dinner you ever had, but you're welcome to it."

Corey grabbed Wayne's hand. "Wayne, come upstairs. I have a surprise for you."

"In a minute, Corey. I want to talk to your mother about something." They went into the kitchen together, and I could hear them talking, but I couldn't make out what they were saying. I edged quietly through the dining room and peeked into the other door of the kitchen just in time to see Mom throw her arms around Wayne. I almost threw up. I sneaked back around the other way and made a lot of noise walking into the kitchen. They weren't hugging anymore when I looked up.

"Wayne!" Corey shouted from the stairs. "I want to show you my surprise."

"Okay, Corey. I'm coming. And your mother and I will have a surprise for everybody later, right, Lois?" He winked at her and she just smiled. I had to force myself not to trip him when he went by me.

Mom pulled the meat sculpture out of the oven. "This is never going to feed everybody." She banged through a few cupboards and tossed me a box. "Here, make this package of macaroni and cheese. We can use it as a side dish."

"Macaroni and cheese on Thanksgiving?"

"Don't give me a hard time, Jenna. The potatoes have grown into a jungle under the sink, so all we have is the meat, cranberry sauce, and a jar of pickles. At least macaroni is filling. I wonder if we should make up the second package?"

The doorbell rang again. When I opened it, there was Vincent, with strands of shocking pink hair sticking out from under his snow-covered ski cap. Little gold icicles covered his beard. "Listen, kid, we just came back for another load, but the plow went by right after we pulled in the driveway, and blocked us in. We've been trying to dig out, but we're freezing. Would you mind if we came in and warmed up for a few minutes? Mrs. Benevenuto's not home."

"That's because she's here. Come on in." They all trooped in, stamping the snow off their boots on the hall rug.

"Mmm. Smells good," Green Hair said. "That your Thanksgiving dinner?"

"Yes," I said. "Did you eat yours already?"

"Naw. None of us have any family around here, so we don't do the turkey bit. We'll grab a few burgers later."

"Smells just like home," Blue Hair said, leaning toward the kitchen. "My ma used to cook a big turkey every year."

Purple Hair licked his lips. "Yeah, mine too, with chestnut stuffing."

They all looked at me, and I could swear I heard their stomachs growling in four-part harmony. "Look," I said, "this isn't exactly a great turkey dinner, but I don't think Mom would mind if you ate with us."

I went back into the kitchen.

"Who was at the door?" Mom asked.

"Vincent and the band. They were freezing, so I invited them to eat with us. I think we're going to need the second macaroni."

"I think we're going to need a miracle," Mom said. She called up the stairs. "Wayne, will you go around and gather up all the chairs you can find?"

Wayne was just coming down the stairs in his

turkey costume, carrying Bruce. Bruce was wearing a costume, too.

"Far out, man," Vincent said. "You guys part of a
group?"

"Wayne says Bruce could be on TV," Corey
yelled. "With Ranger Ralph. Then he wouldn't
have to go to Lollipop Farm. He's going to be—
who is he going to be, Wayne?"

Wayne set Bruce down on the floor. He was
wearing Corey's little Western vest with his tin
sheriff's star badge, and he had on the cowboy hat
from my old Western Barbie doll. "This here's
Deputy Bruce, the traffic turkey," Wayne drawled.
Deputy Bruce pecked at the snow on the rug, and
the hat slipped over his beak.

"I told Wayne how good Deputy Bruce is about
looking both ways before he crosses a road," Corey
said, adjusting the bird's hat.

"Don't get Corey's hopes up, Wayne," Mom said.
"He believes everything you tell him."

"No really, it's true," Wayne said, his wattles
bobbing. "I happen to know that Ranger Ralph has
been looking for a new character to give traffic
safety tips. We conducted a short audition up in the
bathroom, and I think Deputy Bruce here is just
what the Ranger's been looking for. You could make
him a little police costume."

"You mean I'm going to be making costumes for a turkey?" Mom asked.

"You've had plenty of practice," I said. Mom didn't get it for a second. Then she shot me a dirty look.

Mrs. Benevenuto perked up for the first time since the storm started. "Is that the turkey Corey won?" she asked.

Mom nodded. "I'm afraid so. We couldn't bear to have it . . . well, you know."

"Then you had to go out and buy another."

"Well, not exactly. It's a long story, but we're not having turkey for dinner. I made . . . something else." She went into the kitchen and came back with the meat sculpture.

Mrs. Benevenuto peered at it. "It looks delicious, Lois, but do you think it will serve this many people?"

"You made a dish to take to your son's, didn't you, Mrs. Benevenuto?" I asked.

Mrs. Benevenuto's face lit up. "Of course I did. How silly of me. I'll have Vincent help me bring it over. We can heat it up in a jiffy."

While they went for the food, Mom and I put an extra leaf in the dining room table and Wayne rounded up chairs. When Mrs. Benevenuto came back, I realized she had taken the whole band with

her, and each one was carrying a couple of pans.
There was enough food to feed an army. They managed to squeeze everything into the oven but one
huge platter, which Mrs. Benevenuto set down in
the middle of the table. "Here, we'll start with the
antipasto while the rest is heating."

Everyone gathered around the table—four guys
with neon hair, a little old lady whose family didn't
want her, two turkeys that nobody in their right
mind would want, and what was left of our family.
What a bunch of misfits! I couldn't help wondering
what surprise Wayne and Mom were going to
spring on us. I was afraid I knew the answer.
Everything had gotten so far out of control, I
couldn't think of a single thing to be thankful for.

CHAPTER 11

"Minestrone, manicotti, lasagna," Vincent said, piling his plate up in layers. "This is just like a real old-fashioned Thanksgiving at home." For a skinny guy, he could really pack away the food.

"Your chicken and meat-loaf dish is delicious too, Lois," Mrs. Benevenuto said. "You'll have to give me the recipe for it." Mom winked at me and smiled.

"Yeah, getting snowed in here is the best thing that happened to us all week," Green Hair said. "Funny they didn't say anything about the storm on the weather report."

"He's a weatherman," I said, pointing and glaring at Wayne.

Vincent looked up from his plate. "That the name of your group, man? Don't think I ever caught your act. You and the bird do country and western?"

"Jenna means Wayne's a real weatherman—on TV," Mom said, glaring back at me.

"Oh yeah?" Vincent dished himself up some more lasagna with cranberry sauce. "You blew it this time, man."

Wayne tucked his napkin into his neck feathers. At least he'd taken off his beak and wattles to eat. "This storm really took me by surprise. It was caused by a lake effect—you know, the cold air hitting the moisture over Lake Ontario—but the conditions didn't seem right for it. Nobody saw it coming."

"Joseph's goat did," I said.

"Who?" Wayne asked. "Hey, that's right, Jenna. You asked me about a big snowstorm before I left. How did you know about it? Did the guy on Channel Five predict it?"

"No, it was a goat," I said. "Ask Mrs. Benevenuto. Every time Joseph's goat goes into the barn, they get a big storm."

"You wouldn't kid me about a goat, would you?" Wayne said, elbowing Purple Hair. "Get it? Goat? Kid?"

"I got it," Purple Hair muttered. "I think the TV station should hire the goat."

"And fire the turkey," I said.

"Jenna," Mom said, shooting me a look. "That will be enough."

Wayne pretended not to notice what I'd said, but he looked down at his plate as if his feelings had been hurt. I looked at the clock. It was almost three thirty. "What time is it in Colorado?" I asked.

"I don't know, and I don't care," Mom said.

Wayne looked at his watch. "It's two hours earlier than here—about one thirty."

Good. It was still early. Plenty of time for a phone call. Dad probably got up late or something.

The band plowed through the food as if they hadn't eaten in a week, which they probably hadn't. Corey ate a whole pile of manicotti because he thought it looked like eggrolls.

"There's more," Mrs. Benevenuto said, passing the pan of lasagna. "Eat up, everybody. I'll get the dessert ready."

"I couldn't eat another bite," Wayne said, leaning back from the table. "This turkey is stuffed."

Mrs. Benevenuto folded up her napkin and patted it. "We can wait a while for dessert, then. That's what we always used to do at home on Thanksgiving. The seventh inning stretch, my husband used to call it."

She started to clear the table, but Mom wouldn't let her. "You've done enough work for one day, Mrs. Benevenuto."

Corey tugged on Mrs. Benevenuto's arm. "If you come sit on the couch with me, I'll read a book to

you." That was Corey's way of conning somebody
into reading to him. I think Mrs. Benevenuto knew
that, but she gave him a hug and followed him into
the living room.

Purple Hair helped me clear the table. "Too bad
you don't have a dog," he said, scraping the plates
into a big bowl. "He'd have a real feast tonight."

Jaspar! In all the confusion I'd forgotten about
him. "I'll be right back," I said. I bundled up fast
and went outside. It was dark out now, and the
snow was up over my knees where it had drifted
along the side of the house. The gate was still shut
when I got to the back yard, but there was no sign
of Jaspar—not even any footprints. How long had
it been? An hour? Two or three?

"Jaspar," I called. "Here, boy. Here Jaspar!" I
stopped and listened. The only thing I could hear
was the soft sound of a million new snowflakes sift-
ing over the ones that had already fallen. They
sparkled like diamonds under the streetlights, but I
didn't have time to stop and look at them. I struggled down the street, plowing through snowdrifts,
calling into garages, but nobody came. Finally I
gave up and went home.

When I got back to the house, the band was trying to get the van out of the driveway. Three of
them were in front, pushing, and Vincent was driving, rocking the van back and forth. I called to

them, thinking they could help me search, but they couldn't hear over the spinning of the wheels. With a sudden lurch, the van shoved backward through the wall of snow. The other three ran around to the side and jumped in while Vincent gunned the engine. They caught me in their head-lights and waved as they took off down the street. I guess they thought I was just saying good-bye.

Poor Jaspar. He must be freezing. I stumbled through the front door, bringing a pile of snow in with me. Wayne had his whole turkey costume on, and Mom was sewing the headpiece to the neck of the costume. "Somebody will have to cut you out of this after the show," she said. "Jenna, for heavens sake, don't track all that snow in here."

"Jaspar's gone, Mom," I blurted out. "It's my fault. I left him in the yard and forgot all about him."

"He wouldn't go far in this snow," Wayne said. "He's probably holed up in a garage somewhere nearby."

"No, I already tried that. He isn't anywhere."

"I have a little time before I have to be back at the station," Wayne said. "Come with me, Jenna. I'll drive around the neighborhood, and you can watch for him."

Corey was asleep on the couch, curled up with his head on Mrs. Benevenuto's lap. She leaned forward to look out the window. "I hope you find him soon. I hate to think of poor Jaspar running around in this storm."

Wayne put a blue ski jacket over his turkey suit. He looked like an oversized Deputy Bruce. "Why don't just you and I go out, Mom?" I said. "We can look for Jaspar together."

"The garage is completely blocked with snow, Jenna. At least Wayne's car is out in the road. Go along and help him."

We had to brush off the snow before we could even find the door handles, and about a foot of snow slid off the roof onto my seat as I opened the door. When Wayne started the car, the wheels began to spin, but then they caught and we pulled away from the curb. "Leave your window open so you can call to Jaspar," he said. "I'll drive real slow."

"I'm freezing."

Wayne reached into the back seat and grabbed a blanket. "Here, bundle up in this," he said, putting it around my shoulders.

He stuck his head out of his window, calling Jaspar as he drove. I kept hoping nobody would see us, as Wayne's turkey beak vibrated in the wind. "Just let me do the calling," I said. "He knows my voice."

"Two voices are better than one. I think Jaspar knows me."

"All right, he knows you," I said. "But he won't come because he doesn't like you."

Wayne glanced over at me, then looked straight ahead. "I'm sorry you don't like me, Jenna, because I like you. I like your whole family—a lot. Don't you think we could try to be friends, especially now, when Jaspar needs us?"

I stared out of my window and didn't say anything.

"Well, maybe if you're not ready to be friends, you could put your feelings aside and work with me now. How about it, Jenna? A truce, at least?"

I nodded. What choice did I have? I couldn't find Jaspar alone. But was I supposed to put my feelings aside and let Wayne take over our lives, too?

Wayne stuck his head back out of his window. "Jaspar! Here, boy." We drove up and down every street for seven blocks. Once Wayne stopped and backed up because he thought he saw some eyes shining under a tree, but it was just somebody's cat.

We covered the streets all the way to the high school and almost got stuck a couple of times. There was no sign of Jaspar anywhere. My throat

was getting sore from calling, and I was half-frozen
in spite of the blanket. Wayne looked at his watch
again. "I'm going to have to get to the station,
Jenna. I'll drop you off at your house, and I'll come
over to help you look tomorrow morning."

"Tomorrow morning!" I yelled. "What good is
that going to do? You look for a dog right after he's
lost. After that, it's too late."

Wayne pulled up in front of the house. "Look,
Jenna, I'm doing my best. I have to put the
weather report together before air time. You don't
want me to lose my job, do you?"

I jumped out without answering.

Mom met me at the door. "No luck?"

"No luck," I said. "Did I miss Dad's call?"

Mom shook her head. "Jenna, I wouldn't count
on . . ."

Corey came running in from the kitchen. "Did
you find him? Do you have Jaspar?"

I pushed past him. "No, I don't have Jaspar. That
jerky Wayne wouldn't keep looking for him. He
says we'll look in the morning, but that's stupid."

"Jenna," Mom said. "I won't have you talking
about Wayne like that. I was ashamed of the way
you acted toward him today. You should be happy
that he helped you look for Jaspar at all."

"Well, he's stupid to think we can wait until
morning. Poor Jaspar could be dead by then."

"If he is, it's your fault," Corey said. "You're the one who lost him. Wayne was just trying to help."

"Oh, that's just great," I yelled. "Everybody thinks Weird Wayne is wonderful and I'm . . . I'm a big nothing. Wait till Dad calls. I'm going to have a thing or two to tell him."

"Don't be dumb, Jenna," Corey said. "Dad isn't going to call. He never calls. I don't even like him anymore."

I ran up to my room and slammed the door. My room was cold, but I knew it must be even colder wherever Jaspar was. I climbed in bed with all my clothes on and pulled my comforter up around me. I couldn't believe Corey. He was the one who practically fell apart after the divorce. Now he didn't care about Dad at all.

Nobody cared but me.

CHAPTER 12

I heard a knock on my door. "Go away. I don't want to talk to anybody."

"Jenna, I'm coming in," Mom said. She turned on my lamp and sat down next to me on the bed. "I know you're upset about Jaspar, honey, but don't take it out on the rest of us."

"I'm sorry," I mumbled into the comforter.

Mom just sat quietly for a minute. "This has been a pretty unusual Thanksgiving."

"That's one way to put it." I turned my face toward the wall.

"This isn't just about Jaspar, is it, Jenna?"

I couldn't answer.

"Never mind. I think I have some news that will cheer you up. Wayne and I would have made the big announcement at dinner if it hadn't been for all the confusion."

She was going to drop the bomb. She was going to tell me they'd decided to get married. It was all happening too fast.

Mom reached over and turned my face toward her. She looked really happy for the first time in months. "You'll never guess what, Jenna."

I sat up in bed. Maybe marrying Wayne would make Mom happy, but not me. "I don't want to guess. I don't want to hear anything about it. I'm going to look for Jaspar." I jumped out of bed, but Mom caught me in her arms just as I reached the door.

"Jenna, what on earth is wrong with you?"

I struggled to get free. "Wayne is a big fat jerk and I don't want him for a father. I'll run away from home, I swear I will. I'll go live with Dad and Gladys."

"Is that what you think? That Wayne and I are getting married?"

"Isn't that your exciting news?"

Mom let her hands drop from my shoulders. "No, as a matter of fact, it isn't. I can't imagine where you got that idea."

"Oh sure! What am I supposed to think? He's over here so much, he might as well move in, for pete's sake. Besides, I saw you hugging him in the kitchen, so don't deny it."

Mom steered me over to the bed and sat me down. "That's when Wayne had just told me the news. He helped me land a full-time job at the TV station."

"A job? Doing what?"

"As staff artist. Besides doing Wayne's costumes and makeup, I'll be setting up ads, doing public service announcement cards, set design—all kinds of art work." She sat down next to me on the bed. "Don't you see, Jenna? I've finally found a job I can really be good at. We won't be rich, by any means, but my paycheck will cover the bills, and I'll finally be using my talents."

"You're really not going to marry Wayne? You seem to like him so much."

"I do like him. He makes me laugh, and I wasn't doing much of that before he came along. And he's one of the nicest people I've ever met. If you'd give him half a chance, you'd see that he really cares about people."

Just then the phone rang. "That's Dad. I know it is." I ran for the phone in Mom's room. "Hello? . . . Corey, get off the kitchen phone. I can't hear."

"But it's for me!" Corey said. "It's Kevin." I slammed the phone back down.

Mom stood in the doorway. "Who was it?"

"One of Corey's friends," I said.

Mom put her arm around me. "Come on. If

Corey's on the phone, Mrs. Benevenuto is sitting all by herself in the living room."

The Channel Seven News was just starting when we got downstairs. I could see pictures of cars stuck in snowbanks.

". . . worst storm to hit Rochester in over a decade. We'll have a full report by Weird Wayne, WAKY's Wacky Weatherman, after this message."

There was a dog food commercial that reminded me about Jaspar. I opened the front door. A little whirlwind of snow snaked down the middle of the street and disappeared. "Jaspar," I called. "Dinnertime, Jaspar." That always brought him running and barking, but the only sound I heard was the scraping of a snowplow a few streets away.

"Jenna, close the door," Mom yelled. "If Jaspar comes back on his own, we'll hear him on the porch."

The anchorwoman was doing a story about a bank robbery now.

"That's funny," Mrs. Benevenuto said. "I thought they were doing the weather next."

As if answering her, the anchorwoman said, "Weird Wayne will give us the scoop on the weather right after this message."

There was another commercial break, then the sportscaster came on and gave football scores.

"Something's happened to Wayne," Mom said. "I

wonder if I should call the station."

The anchorwoman reappeared in front of the weather map. "And now for the big story of the day. Thirty-six inches of snow dropped on Rochester today, and it's still coming down. Here's what caused it. These big snow clouds right here." She was trying to point at the snow over Lake Ontario, but she missed it by a mile. You could tell somebody off camera was trying to steer her in the right direction.

"What's the matter with her?" I asked. "Even Wayne can get that right."

"It's harder than you think, Jenna," Mom said. "I've seen Wayne do it. She's not standing in front of a map at all. It's just a plain green curtain behind her. When she looks at the monitor, she sees herself in front of the map, and she has to judge where to point. It takes a lot of practice."

"These lines coming down here," the anchorwoman said, pointing way off the map, "are some kind of wind . . . or something. I think they blew the clouds down here from Canada."

"Somebody ought to tell that girl she's got Canada in New Jersey," Mrs. Benevenuto said.

Just then there was some commotion on the porch. I thought I heard a dog barking.

"That sounded like Jaspar," Corey squealed.

Suddenly there was a blast of cold air, and a huge

white turkey and a shaggy, snowy dog burst
through the front door.

"It's Jaspar!" Corey yelled. "Wayne found him. I
knew he would."

"Did they do the weather report yet?" Wayne
asked, breathless.

"They're trying," Mom said, pointing to the TV.
The anchorwoman was groping around for a cold
front.

"I was afraid of that. I'll try to call in the fore-
cast." I watched from the front hall as he ran to the
kitchen phone. "Charlie? It's Wayne. Yeah, I know.
It's a long story. Listen, if you can put me through
over the beeper phone in the studio, I'll do the
weather report from here. Great."

Wayne hung up and started to dial another
number. I went around the corner where I could
see the TV. There were a couple more commer-
cials, then the anchorwoman was back at her desk,
holding a phone. "We have that report from Weird
Wayne now. How does it look out there, Wayne,
and how much more of this snow can we expect?"

"It's still coming down, Phyllis, and we can expect more of the same for the next few hours, until
the wind shifts out of the north. Viewers, if you're
home now, stay there. The city road crews can't
keep up with the snow, and many side streets are
impassable." While the screen showed pictures of

the storm, Wayne went on to explain about cold air over the warm lake and how that pumped the snow in over the city.

"Imagine that," Mrs. Benevenuto said. "Wayne is talking in the kitchen, and his voice is coming out on TV all over the city. Wait till I tell my Tony I was right in the same house with the weather report."

I went back and peeked into the kitchen. The snow on Wayne's tail feathers was melting off, dripping on the floor.

"I'll be back at eleven with a complete weather update. This is Weird Wayne, WAKY's Wacky Weatherman. Back to you, Phyllis." Wayne hung up and grinned at me. "Boy, that was close. This is one Thanksgiving I'm not going to forget."

"Me neither," I said. "How did you find Jaspar?"

He took off his jacket and shook the snow into the sink. "I got stuck on one of the side streets on the way to the studio, so I left the car and kept going on foot. I was calling Jaspar as I went along, when all of a sudden somebody attacked me from behind and knocked me into a snowbank."

"A mugger? In the middle of a blizzard?"

"That's what I thought, but when he started licking my face, I realized it was Jaspar. So I didn't really find him. He found me."

"Thanks for bringing him back," I said.

Wayne shrugged. "Glad I could help." He started toward the living room, nearly tripping over one of his turkey feet. "Guess I really wrecked these things," he said, lifting up one leg with a huge turkey claw at the end of it. "They sure slowed me down in the snow. Driving was pretty tricky, too."

"I bet you left neat tracks, though."

Wayne grinned. "Can you imagine if somebody saw those big tracks in front of their house? It could have started a panic." He spread his wings and did a lurching Frankenstein bird imitation across the kitchen floor. "Monster turkey attacks Rochester."

"Details at eleven," I said, and we both laughed.

"Hey, did your mother tell you the news about her job?"

"Yeah. She's really excited."

"She'll be good at it, too. Your mother's very talented."

"I know." I couldn't think of anything else to say, so I chewed on a jaagged piece of my thumbnail. I wanted Wayne to be horrible and Dad to be wonderful, but now things were getting confusing. I couldn't keep my feelings sorted out anymore.

Wayne sat down on the edge of the kitchen table. "You look kind of sad for a holiday, Jenna. What's wrong?"

Now it was my turn to shrug. "I don't know.

Well . . . yes I do. I thought my Dad was going to call today, and he didn't."

He glanced at the kitchen clock. "Remember, it's two hours earlier in Colorado. Maybe he'll still call."

"Yeah, he probably will," I said.

We were both quiet for a minute; then he cleared his throat. "My dad ran out on us when I was a kid. Did I ever tell you that?"

"Hey, wait a minute. Dad didn't run out on us!"

Wayne held up his hands. "Sorry, that was a bad choice of words."

"It wasn't like that with us. It wasn't the same thing at all."

Wayne nodded. "Well, maybe you're right." He started to reach out to me, then let his hands drop to his sides. "Look, Jenna, I just know what it's like to grow up without a father, that's all. So if you ever need somebody to talk to . . ." His voice trailed off at the end.

I looked at him, sitting there in his stupid turkey suit, and I wanted to laugh and cry at the same time. Dad wasn't going to call. He forgot again. Just like he forgot my birthday, and he forgot to send us money, and he would forget to come visit for Christmas. I'd been the only one who couldn't see that. But sometimes a person has to keep hoping, no matter what.

I looked at the melting snow dripping off Wayne's beak onto his soggy wattles. "You know," I said. "I feel pretty dumb talking to a turkey."

He grinned. "You should see how dumb it feels to *be* a turkey. Come on, I'm going to get your mother to cut me out of this thing."

Mom got up from the couch as we went into the living room. "Wayne, you're a mess. I'm not sure I can salvage this costume for the eleven o'clock news."

"Never mind," Wayne said. "Just get me out of this thing. I think I'll play it straight tonight. Nobody's going to be laughing at today's weather."

Mom cut Wayne out of his turkey costume, then Mrs. Benevenuto served dessert. It was cannolis again, and Corey ate three of them.

"This has been such an exciting day," Mrs. Benevenuto said as I helped her into her coat. "My Tony's house is dull compared to this."

"A circus is dull, compared to this," Mom said.

Wayne put on his jacket. "I'll help you get back to your house, Mrs. Benevenuto. Then I have to head for the studio. It'll probably take me a while to get there on foot." A cold blast of air filled the front hall as Wayne and Mrs. Benevenuto started out.

"Hey, I'll read my library book to you guys," Corey said when it was just the three of us again. "I

gotta do it today, 'cause it's about Thanksgiving."
He climbed up on the couch and snuggled up to
Mom. "I'll let you read it, if you want," he said,
shoving the book into Mom's lap.

Mom brushed the hair back out of Corey's eyes
and smiled. "Jenna?" She patted the cushion next
to her and I settled in, leaning on her shoulder so I
could see the pictures. It reminded me of the times
she read to me when I was little. Corey was smiling
and slowly rubbing his head back and forth against
Mom's shoulder as he listened. At that moment we
didn't seem like three quarters of a family anymore. We were more like three thirds of a family
now, and I'd learned enough about fractions to
know that three thirds make a whole.